ASS

He turned, dropping into a crouch, as the first shot shattered the silence. Clint drew his Colt—swift as silk—and shot his would-be assassin right between the eyes.

In the next second he ducked and threw himself sideways away from the open door as he heard the hostler cry out a warning. Two shots rang out, almost overtaking each other, and the Gunsmith fired again at the movement he sensed more than actually saw in the darkness inside the barn.

A cry of pain and surprise told him his score . . .

DON'T MISS THESE
ALL-ACTION WESTERN SERIES
FROM THE BERKLEY PUBLISHING GROUP

THE GUNSMITH by J. R. Roberts
> Clint Adams was a legend among lawmen, outlaws, and ladies. They called him . . . the Gunsmith.

LONGARM by Tabor Evans
> The popular long-running series about U.S. Deputy Marshal Long—his life, his loves, his fight for justice.

LONE STAR by Wesley Ellis
> The blazing adventures of Jessica Starbuck and the martial arts master, Ki. Over eight million copies in print.

SLOCUM by Jake Logan
> Today's longest-running action Western. John Slocum rides a deadly trail of hot blood and cold steel.

THE GUNSMITH

142

WYOMING JUSTICE

J. R. ROBERTS

JOVE BOOKS, NEW YORK

WYOMING JUSTICE

A Jove Book / published by arrangement with
the author

PRINTING HISTORY
Jove edition / October 1993

ISBN: 0-515-11218-6

A JOVE BOOK®
Jove Books are published by The Berkley Publishing Group,
200 Madison Avenue, New York, New York 10016.
JOVE and the "J" design are trademarks
belonging to Jove Publications, Inc.

PRINTED IN THE UNITED STATES OF AMERICA

10 9 8 7 6 5 4 3 2 1

ONE

From across the wide valley, the horse and rider were almost indistinguishable from the trees and giant rocks that met the bottom of the great sky. Only in movement now as they were silhouetted against the horizon did they become clear to the watching men at the high rim of the box canyon.

But the Gunsmith had already spotted the outriders, even though they were pretty much protected by a thick stand of cottonwoods. For he had caught the sudden flight of the—jay was it?—as it flashed out of the trees; and now in the next breath he saw the glint of sunlight on binoculars.

Shifting in his stock saddle, Clint Adams eased the holstered .45 closer for a swift draw, then loosened the Winchester in the saddle scabbard right by his leg.

"Easy, Duke boy," he said softly, as the big black gelding stomped at a deerfly and tossed his head. "They've more than likely been waiting this

1

while." And he spat over his horse's withers.

Kneeing Duke now, he kept his eyes on the men across the valley, not letting on that he was aware of them as he allowed the horse to find his own gait.

It had been a long ride from Foster's Gap, down south of Split River, and he knew he had still a way to go before he'd reach Landers, Wyoming Territory. He had pushed the big horse for many miles and now wanted to let him rest a bit before they faced this new situation. The Gunsmith had always treated Duke as he would a friend and even now he talked quietly to the horse about what he was aiming to do.

Seen up close, Clint Adams was a lean, muscular man just over six feet, in his thirties, with widely spaced blue eyes, at the corners of which could be seen the faint imprint of crows-feet. He was clearly a man of the big spaces, who could read the weather as well as the land; a man known for swift calculation and action in the face of danger. People said the Gunsmith was nobody to get riled.

All that hot forenoon the man and the horse had followed the thin, hard trail north and west toward the Big Horns. Now, with the sun directly overhead he could feel the heat in the brim of his dusty black Stetson hat as he lifted and resettled it.

As he rode, his keen eyes took in the details of the dry, hard land, figuring how much stock could graze and for how long. He also had to consider the possible danger in the trail ahead. He believed the whole of the Wyoming country was already overgrazed and overstocked, and more than likely it would be picked bone clean soon enough. And likely more sooner than later there'd be big trouble, especially with the railroads pushing so fast into the whole of the west. But that was the way of it as Wayne Behrens had told him. And again Clint's thoughts returned to his friend, the Deputy U.S. Marshal, lying there in bed at Foster's Gap too badly hit by the Spencer rifle that had dry-gulched him to be able to pursue the inquiry into the Blackjack gang, which was apparently operating near Landers and Sunshine Basin. Efforts to get some other lawman to take over Wayne's investigation and bring it to some kind of conclusion had failed. And so Wayne Behrens had turned to his old friend Clint Adams.

At first the Gunsmith had shied at the offer. He'd been a lawman himself some years back, and he'd been real glad to get shut of it. But Wayne was a good man, a friend, and it had burned him to see him lying there on the cot unable to do a damn thing about his situation while no help was sent. Meanwhile, the gang could go on thumbing their noses at himself and the law. Behrens suggested he contact Jake Shore when he got to Landers. Shore was a scout for the Army who was trying to help him clean up the town.

Behrens had told him the gang was located mostly north of Landers. They'd been hibernating for a spell, for in that part of the country, with its crippling winter snows, the holdup business could not be reliable. Highway robbery was definitely not a winter enterprise, not in the high country. But now it was early spring, and Wayne had hinted strongly that the gang was up to something else, something big.

At any rate, Clint had told his friend he would "take a look-see" and then pass on whatever he found—if anything—to the law made up north at Fort Larabee. Within less than a couple of hours after Clint making that promise to his friend, Wayne took a turn for the worse. That night he died.

The Gunsmith shifted again in his saddle, the hot leather creaking, his eyes flicking to the stand of cottonwoods, still some good distance away. But there was no sign of anything. Still, he had that familiar funny feeling. He was all tuckered out to boot, yet that seemed to heighten his perception. He knew he had to be ready for anything.

A bead of sweat rolled onto his eyelid and as he blinked and raised his arm to wipe it away with his sleeve, he caught the glint of sunlight on metal. Suddenly he felt more alert and refreshed than if he'd just awakened from a good night's sleep. Digging his heels into Duke, he ducked low over the saddle horn as the bullet whined across his back and away into the tops of trees.

Too late his eye caught more movement at the stand of pines just east of the trail. Too late he realized that they had him boxed.

He threw himself out of the saddle and started to reach for his .45 while still rolling. The three men were on him before he even had a chance to draw his gun.

"Moved real fast for to of missed you with the Winchester, by God!" The big, stubble-faced man with the very big ears flat against his head stank of tobacco and rotgut whiskey. "Now just where you figger to be headin', mister?"

Clint was on his feet now, swiftly regaining his breath, but he knew he had to stall. He was badly shaken.

"Goddammit! I ast where you was headin' for!"

The man leered right up in front of him and Clint spat at the blotchy red face. As he did, he let his body collapse as though he were falling, at the same time brought his high-heeled riding boot right onto the instep of the man who had been leering at him. Then, without a pause, he twisted again and drove his elbow into the pit of another man's stomach. As he doubled over, the Gunsmith smashed him behind his ear, dropping him like a poleaxed steer. The man whose foot he'd trodden on, let out a scream of pain, while the third man lifted his gun to pistol-whip their potential victim. Fortunately, the Gunsmith was having a lucky day, for the man with the raised gun tripped on a clump of sage and missed his downward sweep with the heavy handgun.

Even so, the Gunsmith couldn't beat those odds, and the three of them—all big and fast—bore him to the ground. His descent was assisted by a singletree smashing him behind his knees. He was on his back now, with a pistol barrel right between his eyes.

"I ast you a damn question, Goddamit!" The man's scraggly beard couldn't hide his flushed, broken face, out of which two small eyes gleamed like polished bullets. He was clenching an unlighted cigar stub between his uneven teeth.

"Chrissake, Harold," another voice said. "Pull the trigger an' let's be shut of the sonofabitch!"

The bearded man spat, aiming nowhere in particular. "You asshole!" he snapped. "You heard the orders!"

"What friggin' orders?"

"What himself given! You deaf or somethin'?"

"But Killigan—"

"Shut up! Shut up, you danged fool!" And the man named Harold wheeled and smashed his companion-in-arms in the guts with his handgun. Then he scratched furiously at his stubbled beard.

It gave the Gunsmith a short breather—very short, but much appreciated. Meanwhile, the victim of Harold's wrath was bent over in agony, trying to curse, but with his breath knocked out he could only croak like an angry frog.

"Lennie!" The man with the gun called to the third man in the trio.

"You want to give him the treatment?" Lennie asked, not taking his eyes from the Gunsmith who was regaining his breath, but pretending to be more hurt than he actually was.

"Himself said no! Don't neither of you shitheads listen to nothin' that's bein' said to you!"

Lennie grinned slyly, looking Harold up and down with loaded eyes as though measuring him for something bad. "You're the boss," he said. "This time out," he added slowly, not taking his eyes off Harold. He turned his head to their companion who was still bent over and vomiting. "You with us, Stacey?" And he chuckled as though his remark had been a particularly funny joke.

Stacey was busy coughing and did not reply.

Harold cocked his tiny eyes at the prisoner. "What you doin' here in this country?" he demanded, sniffing and digging into his ear with his little finger. "What you doin' in this here country?" he repeated.

"I came up here to take a leak!"

His humor was rewarded with a blow in the small of his back.

"Riding through. What's it look like?" And Clint Adams kept his hard eyes right on the man, who had first spoken.

Lennie grinned. "Not through these here parts you ain't, mister. Not here!"

"This is unfenced range, mister," the Gunsmith said.

"Not to the likes of you, it ain't." And Lennie chuckled, looking at his two companions for support. "Not to your likes, by God!"

Stacey, still holding his crotch with one hand, now spoke. "Where you figger to be headin' for, huh?" Stacey's drooping mustache all but completely hid his mouth, and now as he spoke a whistling sound came from his nose.

"Montana," the Gunsmith said calmly.

"Where?"

"I said Montana!"

But before Stacey could say anything, Harold cut in. "That is a long ride, mister. A long ride from here and this ain't the best way. I mean it!"

"It wasn't so bad till you knotheads stopped me," the Gunsmith said, looking at them long and hard.

"You a lawman?" Lennie asked suspiciously. "Huh? He looks like a lawman, don't he boys. And mister, we need a lawman here. Right here. Don't we, boys. I mean, like permanent!" And all three burst out laughing at the weary joke.

"Let him go," Harold said suddenly, and he was laughing as he waved his handgun at their prisoner in dismissal. "He is nothin'. And I mean nothin'!" And suddenly he took a step forward, and poked the gun into the prisoner's ribs. "If we see you again it'll be for your funeral, mister!"

The Gunsmith said nothing. He was remembering what an old gunfighter had told him a long way back; it might have been his old pal Wild Bill. It didn't really matter who. The advice was what needed remembering more than the person. The thing was never to take a situation on somebody else's terms, but to use everything at hand for yourself. "I learned to use what's at hand," was how Bill had put it. "But hell, I know you know that one already."

Well, he did for sure know that one, and he remembered it right now as he stood in front of those three toughs without even a toothpick for a weapon. Hell, they'd even taken his belly gun when they'd braced him. Even so, he considered himself lucky. Something—he had no notion what it could have been—but something in him must

have been expecting trouble ahead. For when he'd
seen a couple of outriders an hour or so earlier just
before crossing the Wood River, and then spotted
a third a few moments later he'd strapped the extra
derringer onto his leg, just below his knee. When
they did brace him and found the belly gun they
figured that was it. Thank God for Mr. Henry
Deringer, he was thinking. Thank God too for
that inner voice that so far had always been there
for him when it got real damn hairy—he had sure
learned to listen to it.

Clint Adams knew exactly what he was going to
do. They had his hand gun, and rifle, *and* the belly gun, thus figuring he was unarmed. The odds
could hardly have been better.

The three were watching him, he noted, but not
too closely, figuring he was stripped. He walked
very slowly toward Duke, faking pain that he no
longer felt.

Very slowly he checked his horse and his saddle
rigging: the bridle, cinch, and his war bag tied to
his saddle skirt.

"C'mon, don't take all day!" The words, coming
from Stacey, were followed by a loud belch.

Good, he was thinking. Impatience was always
an ally when it was someone else's.

Finally, gathering the reins and a handful of
Duke's thick mane in his left hand, he stepped
carefully into the stirrup, swinging his right leg
up and over the cantle. He sat a moment, as
though still in pain, then checked his lariat rope,
reaching to his side away from the three men.
And finally he hitched up his belt.

"I could use my armaments," he said, kneeing Duke closer to the three.

At this all three broke into laughter.

"That is a funny," Harold said. "Account of we could use 'em ourselves."

Lennie was glaring up at him. "Now git!" he ordered. "Git yer ass . . ."

But whatever he was planning to say never got out, for the Gunsmith had suddenly spooked the big black horse. As Duke reared and the three scattered, he reached down to his leg and brought up the derringer.

"Sonofabitch!" Harold's jaw dropped in awe at how they'd been euchred. "Sonofabitch!" he repeated.

"No sir!" snapped the Gunsmith. "The name is not sonofabitch. It is Adams. You are the sonofabitch!" And he kicked Duke in close to the three totally flabbergasted men who were wisely holding their hands well away from their weapons.

"I will take back my guns," Clint said. "And yours to boot." He kneed his horse even closer. "I want all your guns—rifles and handguns!" He had undone his lariat rope from his saddle and now tossed its end down to the men. "You will run the end of the rope through the trigger guards. Got it? All your guns. By the time I get done dragging them halfway to Montana they won't be worth a bottle of cold piss to a one of you. Now git to it!"

It didn't take them long, not under the pressure of their former prisoner's steady gaze. When it was done he kicked Duke into a brisk walk as he dragged the weapons behind him, to the rage and dismay of the three who could only stare in horror and hatred after him. On his way he spooked their horses, which of course didn't make matters any better. It would take them a while to catch the animals.

"Enjoy the scenery," he said with a wicked grin. "I hope for your sakes I don't see you around."

When he was several yards away, and with his eyes on the three, he nudged Duke into a fast canter and headed toward the river.

Those three unhappy guardians of the range could only remain where they were, cursing their former prisoner as he forded the river dragging their rifles and handguns behind him. Their cursing didn't help at all as they witnessed the desecration of the tools of their trade. On the far side of the river, the Gunsmith dismounted and untied their weapons, sufficiently satisfied that they wouldn't be working for a while. Swiftly, he coiled his lariat rope, stepped into his stirrup, and mounted easily.

He was not eager to tarry longer. He realized very well that others would soon be on the scene, those who had been watching all along from the tall timber where he'd first spotted the sun reflecting on those binoculars.

The only question in his mind at this point was whether the trio he'd just flushed were part of the Blackjack gang, or simply outriders for one of the cattle outfits. He'd a notion they were not attached to any outfit based on their abilities at handling livestock. Not cow waddies, that was for sure. And he'd a notion he would find out just who they were soon enough.

There was little question in his mind as to whether or not he would remain a target. In a jiffy the word would spread around the country that there was a stranger riding a big black gelding—a stranger who wasn't any too friendly. Clint Adams knew that somebody would put two and two together and figure the man known as the Gunsmith was about.

And as he pointed Duke toward Landers he knew he was up against something big. And too, he was figuring how it was beginning just the way he wanted it. He was already a target. And he knew from experience that while that was no straight flush, it was still the sort of a hand that saved a whole lot of time.

TWO

"That's him."

Stacey blinked rapidly, as he spotted the horse and rider coming down the main street of the town.

"Who?" It was Lennie asking, while the third member of the trio—Harold—stood just behind them, scratching deep into his wild beard.

"Him what we braced at Morgan's Crossing, for Chrissakes! Who'n hell you think I mean, you stupid shit!"

The boys were standing just inside the window of O'Toole's Marvelous Saloon gazing idly onto the street as they nursed their drinks.

"Christ," snorted Lennie, "Like we was by God expectin' him, setting right here waiting for the sonofabitch to show up."

Whereupon Harold whipped his thick head around, with a sound like a whistle coming out of his twice-broken nose. "Stupid! Don't you never listen to nothin' you get told? I said it a coupla times we'd head here afore himself, taking it short

13

around Squaw Butte and we'd be here waiting. On account of we—I, is what I am saying—on account of myself figgered he wasn't headin' for Montana this good while; the sonofabitch was heading right here for Landers an' I wouldn't mind bettin' what we got on the Lonnergan bank haul that the sonofabitch is up here sniffin' out you know what!"

His hard, steely eyes, now regarded Lennie who had just belched in casual defiance of Harold's authority. Harold's big jaws clamped down hard on the dead stogie which he had not removed in order to speak as he glared at the other man.

Stacey, still blinking rapidly, stepped even closer to the window, as if he could hardly believe what he was seeing. His knobby jaws were chewing vigorously on a plug of tobacco. Unlike his companions, Stacey was almost clean-shaven; his face was shiny, almost orange in color as though he'd spent too much time in the sun without a hat.

He moved closer to the window now, though not crowding either of his two companions. While behind the trio the booming and screeching of the big room continued as though nothing out of the ordinary was happening.

"No!" Harold cracked out the single word as he saw Stacey touch the gun at his hip, flexing his fingers.

"Just figgered to maybe scare the sonofabitch," Stacey said, but there was no apology in his words.

"We got time later," Lennie muttered, his eyes

glued on the horseman as he drew closer.

"An' that's a gut," Harold said, softly almost whispering. His eyes all but bored a hole in the Gunsmith.

Stacey's chewing had speeded up, his hard jaws working faster than a prairie dog's. Then, all at once, he let fly a streak of brown and yellow saliva mixed with pieces of tobacco at a nearby cuspidor. He missed mostly, splattering the wall and the floor and leaving a string of brown spittle hanging down from the corner of his grinning mouth.

"Told us he was headin' for Montana country," Lennie said mournfully, as though he had suddenly lost all faith in mankind. He lifted his eyes to the ceiling above in mollifying prayer, thus bringing the first laughter to their little conclave since they'd lost their prized weapons to the Gunsmith's wanton destruction.

"Mebbe he is." Harold pursed his lips, as if thinking, though it occurred to Lennie that he might simply be smelling his upper lip. At the same time he noted that a certain hardness remained steady at Harold's mouth.

"You figger he's a lawman?" Lennie took a lucifer out of his shirt pocket and began scratching inside his ear with it. Then he popped it into the side of his mouth and began chewing on it. Meanwhile, all three kept their eyes on the horse and rider.

"If he is, he is a dead one. Or as good as." Lennie let his tight face crease into a grin of satisfaction at this attempt at humor.

"Keep your ass out of the winder," Harold warned sternly, speaking with authority over the other two.

"Said he was just riding through on the way north to Montana," Lennie whined, not wanting to leave it alone.

Harold said nothing, his sudden dark scowl showing how rapidly his disapproval had deepened.

The horse and rider were now level with the window.

"Sonofabitch owes us our weapons," Stacey said softly, the words barely escaping his tight lips, his eyes mere slits as he regarded the Gunsmith and his big black horse. "By God, that is hossflesh if I ever seen it. I wouldn't say no to a chunk of that animal, let me say it."

"You mean . . . ?" Lennie shot a glance at his companion, a sly smile taking over his mouth and eyes.

"I do."

"We will wait," Harold said, firm with authority now. "Killigan'll get told. You two knows that, so stash it now."

As the rider moved farther down the street and eventually out of view, a silence held the watching trio. They remained at the window, but still keeping out of view of anyone who might be outside.

"I mind to kill the sonofabitch," Lennie said.

"You figger you can beat me to it, do ya?" Stacey asked sourly. Harold was silent. After a moment his two companions turned to him. "Well, what're we gonna do?" Stacey asked.

"We will kill him," Harold said. "But when me or Mr. Killigan says so." He looked at each of them in turn, staring them down. "I know that man," he said. "They call him the Gunsmith. He is for sure nobody to mess with."

Suddenly Harold turned, as though he had heard someone call his name. There was a deep frown on his face.

"What's wrong?" Stacey asked. "You jumpy, feisty, or the both?"

"Shut up," Harold hissed. His eyes were on the swinging doors as they slapped back against the walls. "He's here."

The three had their eyes on the big man who had just entered. Other heads had also turned, and Felix the bartender reached for a bottle and fresh glass.

He was a giant, and he now turned to the three who were staring at him. He stood a good six feet tall and had a head like a great stone, with small eyes, and thick lips. His face at the moment looked as though it had sometime or other been different. For right now it looked collapsed, which in fact was the result of a dynamite explosion coming within an ace of blinding him during a bank job down in Texas not too many years back.

There was no question about it, Bowdrie Killigan was huge. One day somebody had asked him where he'd originally come from; a dude, to be sure, since no Westerner would have

had the nerve to ask such a question. And Bowdrie
Killigan was in one of his rarer, calmer moods
and replied, "Where do I come from? Mister, I'm
from north of hell!" And he had roared with his
great, giant laughter at the dude's discomfort—it
was always a treat seeing someone else put out.
He slapped the young man on the back, good-
naturedly, yet nearly knocked him to the floor.

Right now his hard, bronze eyes were on
the trio who had been waiting for him.

" 'Bout time you knotheads got back, Goddammit!" And his dark, thick brows looked like a
fence above his eyes as he glared malevolently
at his men.

He paused by them only for a moment. "You
done what I told youse?"

"Sure did," Harold said. "We caught him
right . . ."

But Killigan cut him off. "I'm busy now. I'll
see you after I've had a drink. You meet me over
yonder." And his eyes indicated a corner of the
big, very noisy room.

"That table there with them three?" Stacey
asked.

"Tell them to move! I'll meet you there in . . .
well, when I'm done with my business."

And he was halfway to the bar before the three
fully caught what he had told them to do.

They stood there as he pushed past them, a lane
opening for his passage without his having to say
a word. The Man from North of Hell was no one
to thwart, or to argue with, as the saying went in

Landers and the surrounding country.

The three approached the table finally, after some hemming and hawing as each sized up the situation in his own way. Their decision had been speeded by Mr. Killigan throwing them a look from the bar where he was leaning on his elbows against the mahogany, a drink of whiskey in his hand, surveying the entire room. His eyes lighting on the three sped them to a swift decision, for the two men at the table were not what anyone in that place and time would call "no account." One was a rancher with a spread out on Bonney Creek. The other appeared to be a stock dealer; he looked more "city" than his companion.

Killigan was watching them. They of course knew it was one of his games that he liked to play. He delighted in putting a man in a tough situation and then watching how he handled it, especially those in his employ.

The three knew this; they'd been in such situations before. It didn't make it any easier.

"Harold, you tell them." It was Lennie who came up with this suggestion.

"Shit! Tell 'em what?"

"Tell them the table got reserved," said Stacey.

"Why don't you tell 'em."

"On account of Killigan said for you to do it."

"He sure as hell did not!" Harold was all the way up front in his face with those words, and Stacey almost took a step backward. It wasn't that he was afraid of Harold; Stacey had guts and the three of them knew it. It was that Harold . . .

well, he had a way about him. Somebody'd once told it that Harold had been an officer in the Civil War, though the army he was associated with would be changed in the telling of that information depending with whom one was talking.

"You are supposed to be in charge of us," Stacey said, "leastways that's how you're always putting it, like we have to take orders from you."

"Yeah." cut in Lennie. "We'll take care of that feller what stole our guns and stuff when myself and Mr. Killigan says so . . ." he said, imitating Harold's voice.

"Go screw yerself," Harold said.

"You go screw *your*self!" said Lennie and his voice was loud.

Heads began to turn toward the raised voices of the three men. It was at this point that a disgusted shout came from the bar.

"You goddam assholes stop arguin' right now! You all are annoyin' everybody in this here saloon!"

It was Bowdrie Killigan bellowing at them. "Goddammit. Where the hell you think you're at? I told you to meet me in the back room after I got myself a drink. You dumb shits!" He turned his head and spat swiftly into the cuspidor near his feet. "You dumbbells! Jesus Christ! How'd I get such stupid assholes to work for me?" And he waved his huge arm at them, as though sweeping them across the big barroom and through the door in the corner which led to what was called "The Special Room" by Mr. O'Toole, who ran the place. It was a room for meetings, or for private card games, or even sometimes a dinner. The availability of "The Special Room" of course depended on how much muscle a man could pump. Mr. Killigan never had any trouble getting the room.

The Gunsmith slowly rode the whole length of Main Street, checking the town. He crossed the tracks to the cattle pens and entered the cabbage patch, where at this hour of the morning there was little action other than a single figure at one of the last cribs leaning on the windowsill and watching his approach.

He drew abreast of the shack with its resident sitting at the window, indolently watching him as she smoked. He nodded, not knowing why since he wasn't particularly interested at that time of the morning.

"Hello, cowboy. Come on in and warm up a little." She smiled and winked.

"Not right now," he replied, touching the brim of his hat and drawing rein before turning Duke around to head back up Main Street. "Maybe later."

"No time like the present, hon."

Clint Adams' grin was broad. "That's what I know, lady. But I ain't in the mood right now. Maybe later."

He watched her lips pout, but he could tell she wasn't really offended. "I'll be around," she said, and he noted the slight lisp. "Just remem-

ber I might get busy later. Fact, I know damn
well I will be busy. But I could probably squeeze
you in."

"I'd appreciate that," Clint said genially. And
he suddenly felt something pluck at him. Was it
the lisp?

She wasn't all that good-looking: blond, on the
thin side, maybe in her early twenties. Younger
even? Maybe. It didn't matter. Still, there was
something about her; he didn't know what. Not
wistful, not anything like he felt sorry for her
and her tough life. He knew what nonsense all
that was. She was a tough one, he'd bet on it—
and damn well able to handle herself. Hell, she
had to be in her position. And yet, there was
something . . .

He pulled Duke to a stop and shifted in his saddle to get a closer look at her as she stubbed out
her cigarette. She was wearing a low-cut kimono.

"My name's Clint. What's yours?" he asked.

"Melanie." And she gave a little laugh. "It's my
real name."

He grinned at her, and suddenly realized that
he liked her. "Well, my real name is Clint,'" he
said. And they both laughed at that.

He liked the way her eyes crinkled, and the
way she moved her hands, as though a bit shy.
That realization brought him up short. He'd never met a cabbage patch girl who was shy. But
then the thought occurred to him that maybe
he'd just not been around all that much. Life, by
definition, had to be full of surprises, after all.

"Want to come in?" she asked. "I won't bite you."

He shook his head slowly. "Sorry. Maybe another time." He thought she would move away then, with the conversation finished, but she didn't.

A silence descended. And Duke waited, stomping now and again at a deerfly. One time the big black rubbed his long nose against his outstretched foreleg and his bit jangled, breaking the silence until the girl laughed.

"You look like you've got yourself lost, mister."

"Clint," he said.

"Clint."

"I was wondering if they had a marshal or sheriff in this town. The law. Can you tell me?"

And suddenly he felt just a bit awkward at asking her that question; the law being how it was with her profession. But she smiled pleasantly at him, nodding her head in a certain way she had, and then sniffed and rubbed the end of her nose with the palm of her hand.

"Yonder, stranger!" And she pointed down the street. "On the left, thar!"

And they both burst out laughing at her imitation of his western drawl.

"Reckon that's good enough for yours truly," he said, picking up on it.

"If it's good news then give me credit for showing you the way. If it's bad fergit it." And she nodded her head a couple of times and shot a glance at him to see how he was taking it.

"One more question. Do you know somebody named Jake Shore?"

"Nope. 'Course, the gent might have another name."

"Good enough," he said, touching the brim of his hat in salute to her as he lifted his reins and continued on his way. He felt her watching him as he rode, but he didn't turn around.

It didn't take him long to check out the stock pens, the depot, and what remained of the town. He could see that the stock pens were new, and he had gathered from Wayne Behrens that Landers would be shortly expecting its first trail herd. Well, he figured, things looked about as ready as they were likely to get.

When he rode back up toward the center of town the girl was no longer in her window. Idly, he wondered if she had been called on business.

He still rode watchfully, expecting anything. He was pretty certain the trio who had tried bushwhacking him would more than likely be in town or would appear soon at any rate. He'd taken his time riding in; he wanted to check out the country, the lay of the land. It was his policy on entering any new situation, such as the present one, to first investigate the country, the surrounding outfits, and of course the town itself and the people. For he knew from hard experience that he wouldn't be dealing just with the principals of the event that had called Wayne Behrens into action; there were always what he called "rim people" to watch for. These were people who were not obviously concerned or connected with whatever action was taking place, but nevertheless sometimes played an influential, even important role. They were the men behind the men. For Clint Adams already knew—without

a word having been said by Wayne Behrens—
that the trouble he had encountered as a deputy
marshal had to be only a tiny scratch on the
surface.

He rode with care now, seeing everything, yet
without turning his head much. Just like any man
seasoned to the hard trail and hairy town he knew
that you could take in a lot more if you didn't let it
be known you were looking. The main thing was
not to get so caught up in what you were looking
at. And that you'd be an easy target. More to the
point, never get caught with your pants down.
That was the time you got it, but in spades. Clint
Adams had learned that lesson early, while he
was still a button. He had some good teachers
back then, and later he learned even more rubbing shoulders with his pals Wild Bill Hickok,
Bat Masterson, and a few others: men who understood very well that the most important thing in
a gunfight was to stay alive.

He had indeed spotted someone watching him
from the big saloon, and it crossed his mind that
it could be the trio who had tried to whipsaw him.
On the other hand, it could have been somebody
simply sizing the weather.

He could see right off that Landers was all he'd
heard it was: lively and, if a man wasn't any too
careful, deadly. Old Pony Creek Tom Rickett had
put it that Landers was a town where a man
couldn't always be sure that he wouldn't like it
so much he'd end up staying there permanently—
courtesy of lead poisoning.

The hitch racks were crowded, as he'd expected, so he decided on .the livery.

The old-timer hostler—evidently a bronc stomper who'd gotten stove up and had to quit—greeted him sourly from around his full chew of plug tobacco.

"I'll pay extra for your taking special care of him," Clint said as he dismounted.

"Why?" The old boy snapped back like a coyote aiming for a special morsel. "You figure the hosses don't get good enough service in this here hotel? But I will accept your extra money even so," he added swiftly. "Just don't cotton to a young feller such as yerself gettin' wrathy."

But the Gunsmith was suddenly not in the mood for banter. Something had caught his attention in the farthest corner of the livery barn. Some kind of movement.

"It'll be Jesse," the liveryman said, sensing what the problem was. "He's my dad. Going on a hundred and one, by jingo. He don't see so good and now and again he runs into somethin' or somethin' runs into himself. Any case, there's a jangle. Sounds to me like he run into that stack of spruce just out back of the barn." Then, raising his voice to a shout. "You all right there, Paw?"

A pause, while Clint wondered would there be an answer, or simply silence. And then a feeble cackling; "Got these goddam logs right here in my path, fer Chrissakes! What'n hell, you tryin' to get rid of me, boy?"

"Old feller's a bit tetched, just now an' again."
And with a great hawking, he let fly at a scampering pack rat, missing him easily. "Shit take it,"
he muttered, easy as remarking the time of day.

"I'm still paying extra," Clint said, coming back
to the subject of Duke's stay in the livery. "I'll fork
him some hay, and you can grain him. Make it a
half a can."

"He eat with a fork and knife, does he?" The
old man's tone was sour as a lemon.

"You could ask him if you've a mind to," Clint
said, dry as a bone. He grinned to himself as he
ran his hand between Duke's twitching ears. "See
you by-an'-by, Duke boy."

"Jesus," muttered the hostler.

"I don't want anyone coming near him," the
Gunsmith said, his voice hard as nails. "I am
paying for that too. Remember that."

"I will remember that, mister." And suddenly
he wasn't funning anymore.

Clint stood for a moment looking again at the
old man, studying him as though he wanted to
remember him in detail. Which, in fact, he did.

"I will be back in an hour, maybe two."

"He is prime horseflesh, mister. No question
on that. But shit, even the Queen of Sheba don't
deserve that much bullshit, fer Chrissakes." The
old man had returned to his sour tone, as though
afraid he'd been showing weakness.

But the Gunsmith answered him in the best
possible way; he simply ignored the remark. And
the silence fell into the barn like a bad smell,
reaching into all the corners, cracks, and crevices.

Like a lot of horsemen, the Gunsmith never walked even a few yards if he could ride, but in this instance he wanted Duke to rest and catch up on himself. It had been a long, tough ride up from Foster's Gap, even without the interruption of the three hard cases.

He was aiming for the center of town, having spotted a sign as he rode in that said GENERAL STORE. This false front building—like so many others in such towns—looked as though it had been grown right out of the sagebrush that abounded. It had the strange attitude of appearing sturdy and at the same time gave the impression of imminent decay.

A heavyset gent, whose baggy pants were supported with yellow galluses plus a wide leather belt, nodded as he entered.

"I am needing some ammo for the Colt and Winchester, both," Clint said, approaching the beat-up wooden counter.

The storekeeper's eyes flicked to the customer's holstered .45. "For the Colt . . . hmm." The tone was friendly, but the Gunsmith heard more in it. He kept a close look on the other man. The storekeeper's oily, thin black hair was combed flat against his bullet-shaped head. Clint noted that the man's hands were puffy, as he placed one on the counter and that there was no indentation between the knuckles.

"Two boxes each for now," Clint said. "Two for the Colt and two for the Winchester .44-.40."

"New to the country, are you?" the storekeeper asked pleasantly. He was an enormous man with loose folds of skin hanging from his face; it was as though his body was enclosed in a sack that was too big. He flushed a little as Clint paid the money and didn't answer him.

The Gunsmith—like any man of the West— was immediately on guard with a man asking questions. He had the feeling that the storekeeper wasn't just being nosey. He wore a frown on that big face, and was obviously not happy.

Then he saw the big man's eyes flick to the door behind him. A thin, nail-hard man had just walked in wearing tin on his hickory shirt. Clint caught his reflection in the mirror on the wall behind the storekeeper.

It had always been the Gunsmith's habit when arriving in a town where he wasn't known to visit the law—either sheriff or marshal—just to let the representative of law and order know that he was about. But in this instance as he was riding on down to the livery he had seen the shade drawn on the door of what was clearly the lawman's office, indicating that the premises were closed, and that no one was about.

The storekeeper had pushed the boxes of cartridges across the counter and Clint had put down money. As he did so he turned and faced the stern-faced representative of law and order in Landers.

"The name is Steiner. Sheriff Ed Steiner. I am letting you know that for your own protection in Landers, and for the protection of anyone else you might run up against. Meanin'...." And he threw his thumb towards the tin badge on his shirt. "I am the law."

"My name . . ." Clint started to say, but the lawman cut him off.

"I know yer name. I am giving you fair warning, mister. You cause any trouble in Landers and you'll have myself and a dozen deputies to face off on." The voice was hard, the voice of a man laying down the law, the Gunsmith noted.

"I am not here to make trouble, I'm not even looking for trouble, Sheriff," Clint said easily, facing the other man squarely, still holding the boxes of ammo in his hands. "I saw your office was closed when I rode in; otherwise I would have stopped in on you like I generally do when I hit a town where they don't know me."

"We know each other now," the marshal said, not giving a country inch.

"I do appreciate your hospitality, Sheriff," Clint said with an amiable grin. "I've ridden up from Foster's Gap, on behalf of my friend Wayne Behrens. You likely know him. Marshal Behrens."

"Never heard of him."

Marshal Ed Steiner leaned forward now, and his hand touched the gun at his hip. "I'm letting you keep your gun, mister. But I'll have my eye on you."

It was on the tip of Clint Adams' tongue to tell the sheriff how "cozy" that would be, since he's already seen a half dozen armed citizens about, but he restrained this sudden burst of acid humor and simply nodded. Steiner must have figured he would never give up his gun. At the same time he was pretty damn sure Steiner did know of Wayne

Behrens. The lie had been clearly evident in the speed of his denial.

When the lawman had left, Clint waited a moment. Then, with a nod in the direction of the storekeeper, he started toward the door.

"Quiet in town," the storekeeper said, trying to pick up where he'd been interrupted by the marshal's appearance. "Course it'll be a whole lot livelier come the Fourth. Landers always does it big on the Fourth of July. This year we're lookin' to have some rodeo stuff. Should be somethin'."

The Gunsmith stopped and turned then, facing the big man with the loose skin that seemed to be hanging off his face and neck and forearms. "I am looking for a man named Shore, Jake Shore." He was looking closely at the other man, reading his reaction to the name. "Know him, do you?"

The words were both question and simple declaration, and he could see the heavyset man wasn't ready for it.

"Should've ast the sheriff," he said, carefully defensive. "You could catch up with him. More'n likely he is headed for his office." And he threw his thumb in the direction he was meaning. "Reckon you figgered where that is." And he ran the tip of his tongue quickly along his upper lip and scratched his crotch. His nervousness was not lost on the Gunsmith who was reading him closely.

The Gunsmith turned to go.

As he put his hand on the brass doorknob, the storekeeper said, "I'm Hogarth Petersen. And this here is my business, my store." He let a little laugh mixed with an unexpected cough pop out of his tight face. "Want you to know you're welcome here, mister. A pleasure to do business with you." His small eyes dropped to the boxes of cartridges, and then back up to the Gunsmith's face.

"Good enough then." The Gunsmith gave a nod as he opened the door and stepped out onto the boardwalk.

Hogarth Petersen stood in the doorway. "Didn't catch your name, mister."

Clint Adams looked directly at the man, taking in the sloping shoulders, the potbelly, the sagging trousers. And he realized that there had been something strange in the way the storekeeper had replied to his question concerning Jake Shore. "Don't believe I dropped it," he said.

He started to turn away again, but realized that there was something he was missing. He was still thinking about the way the storekeeper had responded to his inquiry about Jake Shore. He turned back to face the man, and saw the color coming into those loose cheeks.

"Tell me what's happened to Shore," he said softly. "Is he still about?"

"In a way of speaking, he is that."

"You're saying he is dead?"

"Right now Jake Shore is in heaven or hell— take your pick."

THREE

When the Gunsmith sat down in the chair left empty by the drummer from Denver, the dealer broke out a fresh deck.

"It'll be straight draw," he said, pulling the joker.

The dealer was a small man: short, bordering on tiny, but his hands were lightning, as the Gunsmith instantly noted. His name was Three-Finger Titus, for the evident reason that he had lost the fourth and fifth fingers on his right hand. Clint Adams noted how he had turned his accident to excellent advantage. Three-Finger was incredibly able with his diminished hand and indeed, he had clearly been helped by the missing fingers—or so it appeared. He handled those cards like they were his very own limbs a part of him.

It took almost no time at all for the Gunsmith to peg what Three-Finger was up to. So why not? he thought. Card playing was serious business. And the Gunsmith quickly saw that Mr. Titus knew his business not only backward and forward, but sideways and upside down, and however else a man wanted to describe it. It was, for the Gunsmith, a pleasure to watch such a pro at work.

And he quickly saw that Three-Finger understood very well the most important principle involved in playing cards—and winning: the study of the players themselves. The players were in fact the game. It was like gunfighting. A gun was only a gun, but the main question—indeed, the only question—was who was holding it.

For some while now, the Gunsmith had more or less drifted along with the action, studying the men at the table, their habits, the little giveaway comments and gestures. For he had learned early in life that you never found out much about people meeting them in church. He knew that if you studied poker you could learn a good deal about men, and about gunfighting, since both endeavors required only two kinds of people— winners and losers. And here at O'Toole's Marvelous Saloon he had the perfect opportunity. Liquor was his ally here; booze the great tongue-loosener.

When he had entered quietly, he could tell instantly that his presence was already known in Landers. It was nothing anybody had said, naturally, but more what was not said. Nor had there been any special looks. It was atmosphere that tipped him off to the climate, and he felt like he almost knew what the little dealer was going to do next. Clint Adams had discovered early in life that learning one thing could more likely than not teach you something else; even something very different. But only if you understood the principle.

The smart gambler always looked for the other player's giveaway. And fairly early in the game the Gunsmith spotted Three-Finger Titus's. Whenever the little dealer was bluffing, he sniffed before taking a card or announcing his bet.

Until just now there hadn't been much life in the game. Three-Finger dealt with skill, his pasty white hands flashing under the light of the coal-oil lamp which was on even though it was still daytime outside. On the fourth deal Clint opened for the usual ten dollars, on a pair of aces. He was sitting to the dealer's right. Three-Finger raised him twenty. Clint stayed and drew three cards.

Three-Finger's smooth, innocent face turned into a knowing smile. He sniffed and said, "I play these."

The Gunsmith didn't help the aces. He knew what was coming but wasn't sure just what he would bet. He caught Three-Finger glancing at his chips, figuring how much he had left. And then he bet fifty dollars.

The Gunsmith pretended to hesitate. "I call," he said, after a rather lengthy silence and spread his hand, face up, showing two aces.

Three-Finger Titus couldn't conceal a look of total disbelief. "I'll be hung out to dry, by God," he snapped and threw his hand face down in the discards. "Didn't you know I stood pat?" he snorted in disgust. "Goddammit, how'n hell can you call a pat hand on two aces?"

The Gunsmith's smile was just barely there. "It wasn't all that hard," he said, remembering how Three-Finger had sniffed. And looking around at the careful faces he knew that he had scored the extra he'd been aiming for. Now the big game would begin.

Not only Three-Finger Titus, however, was aware of the stranger's poker-playing acumen. The other players at the baize-top table knew it as well as Felix File, the bartender. Indeed, all in that crowded room were well apprised of the stranger's speed, accuracy, determination, and by-God guts. Walking into a poker game like that! With no less than Titus himself whipsawing the action! Something to smoke in your pipe, that was!

And now he was at the bar. Adams was the name, and the word "Gunsmith" was heard muffling through the stirring crowd at O'Toole's Marvelous Saloon.

And that was just what the Gunsmith wanted: his presence known. How else would he attract the information he was after? It was the stickiest game, nonetheless, for the risk was enormous and, if it ran against you, final. Clint Adams was deliberately counting on the character of the man or men he was after. He'd been around the West and its dangers long enough to know that the most difficult thing to hold on to was a secret. And the most interesting thing about this particuliarity of the human character was that the bigger and the more dangerous the secret, the more likely it would leak. After all, as the Gunsmith well knew, a secret was like money, and a big secret indeed was big money. Of course, he realized he was at risk, and that the risk grew in proportion to the power of the secret.

As he walked down to the Wrangler's Rest Hotel where he'd taken a room, he was sure that he was being watched. And in fact he appreciated the swift reaction of whoever it was that had singled him out so quickly. Well, after all, he had stated what he wanted loud and very clear—to Sheriff Ed Steiner, to Hogarth Petersen in his general store, and yes—by golly, he'd almost forgotten— to the girl in the cabbage patch—what was her name?—yes. Melanie. But beyond that, he was now pretty damn sure that somebody had sent word ahead from Foster's Gap. Otherwise, how come those three had tried to bushwhack him? He simply could not accept the possibility that they were outriders just doing their duty for one of the big outfits in the high country. He knew that he'd been backtrailed since he'd left Wayne Behrens back in Foster's.

And now when he walked into the Wrangler's Rest and saw the room clerk he knew he had company.

The man behind the desk nodded, averting his eyes as though searching for the room key, which was in its obvious slot, and close at hand. Finally, he found it. Clint noted that he was more than wary, even beyond nervous.

He was in fact frightened—the Gunsmith could see this clearly. He must have been in his sixties,

and he almost dropped the key as he laid it on
top of the desk, doing his best to avoid the Gunsmith's steady look.

"Howdy," Clint said, his tone not unfriendly.

"Howdy." The word came out in a whisper,
and the red-rimmed, coffee-colored eyes fumbled
around, not knowing where to look. Well, whoever was running the show, the Gunsmith decided, they'd caught a weak spot here.

Or had they? Suddenly it swept into his mind
that perhaps his reaction to the old man at the
desk had been anticipated. But toward what purpose? Why would someone want him to be on his
guard? Usually in such events as this the aim was
to get the mark off guard.

But he had already picked up the key, not wanting to linger at the desk unnecessarily. Then on
an impulse, he reached over and turned the room
ledger around, and checked it.

He started toward the stairs and then abruptly
swung on his heel and said, "Who's up there in
my room?"

The clerk turned pale and pretended to cough.
He then took advantage of the interruption to pull
out a big blue bandanna and began to hawk and
spit into it. It almost covered his red face, while
he was obviously trying to marshal a reply to
the hard man standing there on the other side
of the desk.

"Sir, mister—it ain't my fault. They just come
in and . . ." He stopped, his eyes darting to the
stairs leading to the floor above. "And . . . told me
I better . . ."

He stopped, overcome by a real attack of coughing.

"Who's up there?" Clint repeated when the coughing subsided. The man's sweating red face looked at him over the edge of the blue bandanna that he was holding to his mouth.

"How many?"

For a moment he though the old man wasn't going to answer him, but then the bandanna dropped as he lowered his hands and the words stumbled out.

"They ain't there now. They was two men an' . . . an' a young woman. The men, they came down after about five minutes and left." He was shaking. "They told me not to say nothin'. They said I'd be sorry if I did. Real sorry. . . . Mister, don't tell. Don't tell . . ."

"Two men and a woman."

The old man nodded. He was terrified.

"And they just came back down after two–three minutes and left?"

"Mister, that's the God's truth, so help me!"

"All three left?"

The eyes which had been pointing toward the stairs now swung toward Clint Adams. "The—the men come down. The woman, she stayed up there. Leastways, I didn't see her."

"She could have slipped out?"

"Maybe. Mister, those men. They were scary, you know what I am meaning. . . . An' maybe she was with them and I just didn't . . . didn't notice like. Mister, I'm an old man and I don't want no part of Bowdrie Killigan's boys."

Clint Adams studied on it a moment, his eyes on the top of the stairs. He was also fully aware of the rest of the lobby of the hotel, and mindful too of how a story of this nature could grip a man to the point where he'd forget himself and be a setup for a beating, a bushwhacking or whatever . . .

"Mister, I am tellin' you the God's honest . . ."

Clint had turned away and was now quickly and silently mounting the stairs. He could feel the old man watching him. Another part of him was wondering whether someone else was also watching.

His room was at the end of the hall, with a window facing onto an alley. It was dark in the hall, though he had no trouble in seeing his way. No light came from beneath the door. And the thought flashed through his mind that a third man might have been placed somewhere upstairs before the other two came with the woman, with the room clerk not noticing. But it was thought only at the edge of his mind and he was intently studying the door right there in front of him. No light, and no sound. He had good ears, the Gunsmith, and he also carried that extra sense that had stood him in such good stead on the trail—and in towns too—these past years. He was pretty sure there was someone in the room, though he caught no sound of movement. Not even breathing could be heard as he pressed his ear to the door itself.

Then he stepped slightly back and stood very still, aware of his own body, its life, its breathing, its looseness, and its tightness in the various necessary places. In short, he listened with his whole body. A Shoshone Indian had taught him that some years back. And he had grown it over the years, that very special ability in listening with the whole of himself.

And yes. Someone was in there. There was not a sound, not even the sound of somebody breathing on the other side of the door. There was only silence, utter and complete. Yet he knew it wasn't so. He could feel someone there.

He stepped back now and checked the hall, both ends. He wanted to be sure there would be no one coming at him from another room.

He waited, still listening. And then he heard a movement in the room. Stepping to the side of the door frame, with his hand close to his holstered six-gun, and ready for the draw, he took his key in his other hand and pushed it into the lock.

At that point the door was pulled open from the inside and he could smell her.

"Don't shoot," said a familiar voice. "I'm just going to turn the lamp up so we can see each other better.

"Surprised?" Melanie's eyes were laughing with pleasure.

"Pleasantly so. Yes," replied Clint with the sudden warmth flowing through him as he saw the firm snow-white curve of both breasts bursting almost right out of her dress. More than that, he could feel the power of her lust and his own rising between them.

But the Gunsmith was no damn fool. He resisted

heroically, walking to the window and checking it. There was no balcony outside, no chance for sudden and unexpected entry. And there was no one to be seen in the alley below.

"You're not expecting company, I hope," Melanie said.

"Just being careful." He stood away from her and she pouted.

"You're angry at me."

"I want to know what you're doing here. And he could feel his erection pressing hard as a club against his pants. It got even harder when he saw her eyes drop to look at it.

"That's quite a weapon you've got there, sir."

"I'm asking you how come you're here."

"I wanted to see you. I—I've sort of fallen for you, sir."

"Save it for the eagles, lady. Now you better get going. I'm busy."

Suddenly she sat down on the edge of the bed and, dropping her head into her hands, began to cry.

For a moment he thought she was faking it, but when he caught the sound of sniffles and heard her actually sobbing he realized something was indeed different than the old ploy of luring him into a trap.

"I didn't want to come," she sobbed. "But they made me." And she lifted her head, the tears running down her cheeks.

"Who? Who made you? And why?"

"I told them, I begged them not to make me come. But they said they'd have some men beat me. I've seen what they can do. I saw what they did to Betty, my friend. They blacked both her eyes. Oh God . . . Oh my God . . . !"

And she was sobbing now in his arms. He held her loosely, for he still wasn't sure. If she was lying then he had to admit she was a damn good actress.

"I liked you mister. When I first saw you. But they—they came just after you left. They must have seen us together."

"Who?"

"Two men." She wiped her eyes. "First they began pushing me around my room. I'd thought they had come for—well, business, like. Oh, my God . . . they were awful, horrible."

"What did they want you to do? Set me up, huh?" And his eyes went to the door which he had carefully locked.

"I don't know their plan. Maybe, maybe when we were in bed they'd break in. And . . . and . . ." And she started to cry again. He put his arm around her shaking shoulders.

"What are you gonna do?" she asked, controlling her tears with difficulty.

He stood up and looked down at her. "I want you to stay right here. I'll be back in a couple of minutes." And he opened the door and stepped out into the corridor.

"What—where are you going?" She was standing just inside, keeping herself behind the door.

"We're moving," he told her.

"What do you mean?"

"We're taking another room."

"But—but where? Is there a room vacant?"

"I took a quick look at the desk clerk's ledger when I signed in. Like I generally do when I check into a hotel. There are some rooms vacant on this floor."

"But—but do you have a key?"

He grinned at her concern. "I'm a pretty good lock picker," he said. "We'll try number five down that way. I checked it out when I checked in this afternoon."

She smiled at him then, and it widened into a grin. "I figured you for a smart one when I first saw you, by golly."

"Good enough. Now let's get out of here. We'll leave the light on and lock it."

In only a couple of minutes they were in another room at the other end of the hall.

"We'll have to be real quiet," he told her as he locked the door behind them and wedged a chair under the knob.

She was grinning at him, her eyes shining.

"Mister, I can sure see you weren't born yesterday."

The Gunsmith reached over and patted her check gently as they stood beside the bed. "And remember this—I wasn't born today either," he said.

Almost before he knew it she had stripped and was inside the bedcovers, her face small and very quiet on the pillow, with the light from the coal-oil lamp reflecting on her blond hair. Her eyes were closed, but then as he shucked off his shirt

and dropped his pants she opened them, staring
with fascination at his erection as he turned down
the lamp.

"You want it dark or light?" he asked.

"I want you," she said, and she threw back the
covers as he climbed into the wide bed.

His hands instantly found her body, slipping
down her back and onto her already undulating
buttocks while he thrust his rigid member between
her eager legs.

"God, I want it," she gasped and, reaching down,
grabbed his hard cock and began stroking. He was
already slick, and her hands was marvelous. Still
stroking, their mouths met and their tongues min-
gled and sucked at each other as his hand moved
to her bush, which, too, was wet.

"Oh, my God, I have to have it!" And she was on
her back, her legs spread as he mounted her, driving his great cock deep and high, touching bottom with it and stirring it round as she gasped
and pumped her buttocks with his in an increas-
ing rhythm.

Faster and still faster, and deeper, and higher,
and this way and that and this and that and . . .
and . . .

"My God," she whispered into his ear. "You
came a fucking gallon!"

The Gunsmith was hardly able to speak. But
being a gent at heart he managed. "I do my best."
And he nibbled lightly at her earlobe. "You're not
so bad yourself, young lady."

"I do my best." The words came out breathily,
for she was still gasping.

They lay together silently. He listened to any possibility of sound out in the hallway. But only silence came back to him.

He didn't dare sleep, though he would have liked it. Always after a good bout in bed he enjoyed a light snooze. And he could hear the girl's breathing change, as though she were slipping towards sleep.

But then he felt her hand on his balls, and she snuggled closer to him, raising her leg and covering him with her thigh, as she continued to play with him.

His erection sprang to life, lifting the sheets into a pyramid of joy.

"God, what a lovely cock!" she whispered. And the next thing he knew she was down on him, taking his rigid stick right down her eager throat. Then they released each other so he could mount her, bearing the unbearable for the second of agonizing separation.

He had his hand covering her bush, his middle finger probing deliciously into her soaking cunt, finding the button and teasing it as she squirmed and gasped, and at one point she started to cry out, though he caught her just in time with his hand over her mouth.

"Shh! For God's sake, you'll have the whole house in here, not to mention those knotheads who tried to set us up."

And then she was crying, weeping on his shoulder, and squeezing his balls, and wrapping her leg around him. "I'm sorry. Oh, I'm sorry . . ."

He squeezed her with the arm that was around

her shoulders, and tickled her ear with his tongue.

And for a moment or two they lay there quietly without moving. But then her hand slipped to the crack in his ass and began tickling up and down as his member rose to an even greater rigidity than before.

And she was down on him again, pumping her head up and down as she sucked and sucked . . . all the way, taking it as far as it would go down her throat, and bringing it right out to just behind its head as her tongue sucked and sucked.

Clint Adams knew he couldn't stand another second of it, and then he was pulling her up and she mounted him, lying on top, pumping up and down on his bone-hard member until he couldn't stand another second of it. Nor could she as she rode him plunging up and down and wiggling as the head of his cock ground into the wall of her begging vagina.

And together they came and came as she gasped in utter ecstasy, begging for more and more and more . . . until it was enough, more than enough.

They lay supine on the bed, spent, wrapped up in their joy and utter satisfaction.

The Gunsmith realized that he had seldom equalled, and never surpassed such a moment.

They lay there, arms holding each other. And after a moment he heard her breathing change as she fell asleep.

He lay there listening, while the girl beside him slept.

FOUR

The End of the Journey Hotel and Prime Lodging sat like a very loud example of what travel writers were calling "western hospitality" in their books and pamphlets and newspaper articles. Three stories high, it took up the equivalent of nearly three other buildings in space. Somehow, although it had been put up in haste—as so many of the town's houses and stores—somehow it managed to give the impression of a certain durability, even confidence. But—as one writer pointed out—that might have been because of the excitement of its gambling room, dance hall, and dining facilities, not to forget its large, expensively appointed meeting room, plus two smaller ones.

The dining facilities were first-rate with good service, and good food. By and large The End of the Journey was considered in that part of the frontier as a fine place to catch up on something other than the customary meat and potatoes, man-killer whiskey, and wine that tasted like it had never seen a grape. At any rate, the place was relatively new, and quite successful thanks to the endeavors and patronage of some well-to-do cattlemen, who held regal sway in that large section of the Wyoming Territory. More especially, thanks to the presence—and foresight—of Mr. Cecil Dunbellamy, The End of the Journey was doing very well indeed.

Presently, the "A" meeting room was hosting the attention of Mr. Cecil Dunbellamy himself, plus five leaders of the community: Calhoun Worth, president of the Landers National Bank; Tyson Pettiford, likely the richest stockman in the area; Hogarth Peterson, owner of the town's biggest store; Fifield Wister, publisher, editor, and owner of *The Landers Bugle*, the weekly newspaper; and finally, the law itself in the person of Ed Steiner, town sheriff.

The group—with the exception of Cecil Dunbellamy—were considered as representing Landers in political and financial decisions. Known as "them that carried the money," no one held any special political office, such as mayor. Indeed, the inhabitants of Landers seemed to take pride in the fact that they had no mayor. It might have been this attitude that had contributed in perhaps a small way at least to Mr. Dunbellamy's choosing Landers for his . . . operation. Or, maybe the men behind him in Chicago had other reasons for the choice. But these thoughts were not in any way paramount in the reflections of the present half dozen "community leaders," as Fifield Wister was already calling them

in his mind as he planned his next editorial enti-
tled "The Future of Landers in the Coming History of Wyoming."

Cecil Dunbellamy, at the head of the table, had
allowed several minutes to elapse while the gentlemen settled into their chairs, had their first taste
of the beverage that Mr. Dunbellamy was serving,
and in general eased into the meeting.

"Gentlemen, I am reasonably sure that you all
know why I have asked you here this afternoon,
at least in a general way. For you well know how
interested I am in the future of our country, the
Wyoming Territory, and especially Landers, a vil-
lage, a town—possibly one day a city—which I
feel dear to my heart."

Mr. Fifield Wister had turned rather glassy-eyed
hearing these noble words, and wondered how
many times the speaker had previously uttered
them in meetings with people whom he planned
to use for his own purpose or, at any rate, for
his company. Fifield Wister was no yokel and
he could smell what he called the "gull" being
set up. His expression however, revealed nothing
but earnest attention for his host. Meanwhile, he
was trying to remember what and where he had
heard something very interesting about Mr. Cecil
Dunbellamy.

On the other hand, Hogarth Petersen was feeling marvelous, basking in the knowledge that
someone very important was courting his favor
with great benefit to his business. Tyson Pettiford,
the stockman, and Calhoun Worth, the banker—
and in his own very personal opinion "financial

wizard"—were both hanging onto every word that came from the lips of this man they had heard such a good deal about. To be sure, none of those present, knew or even suspected that Cecil Dunbellamy's arrival in Landers—which had been presented so casually as an overture from the Northern Pacific—had been planned meticulously. The timing, the living arrangements, and not to forget the dossiers on all those present at the table were all part of the plan. Dunbellamy was not a man to overlook details. He prided himself on being a very intelligent man, and a strong man moreover, because he never—*never*—allowed loose strings to be left around that could trip him.

"Gentlemen, I am, as you know, very concerned about the future of the Great American West . . ." A pause, with a careful smile touching the thin lips. "Of course, I am only a humble admirer of the frontier. I am not a long-time resident such as yourselves, but I love the West and especially this particular area—Wyoming. Wyoming with its great mountains, rivers, valleys, and plains—and men. Gentlemen: it is the men of the great West who have built this great country and it is this same caliber of men that will assuredly continue to do so." He paused, reached for his glass of whiskey, and drank. His listeners followed suit.

"Gentlemen, as you realize the whole situation in the West has changed—and changed radically—almost wholly in consequence of the Great Railroads and the great numbers of immigrant peoples pouring in from the many nations of Europe. The influx—I have been told, and I assure you it is true—the influx of people who are westward bound is enormous. The railroad is opening up a new era, indeed, a completely new century in American history!" And his hand swept to his glass.

In the next moment he was on his feet, his glass raised. The others swiftly followed suit, though Hogarth Petersen's foot kicked the leg of his chair, nearly upending it. Then, reaching to save what might have become a serious accident Hogarth—not the most graceful man in the world—knocked into Tyson Pettiford, a man of sour temperament, which he directed very much toward tradespeople. However, the moment did not turn into an incident. And Cecil Dunbellamy held his glass firm, his arm raised, eyes directed toward the amber liquid which had picked up the light from the coal-oil lamps and reflected it—giving C.D., as he called himself in his thoughts, a rather good feeling.

Seated again, and after the waiter had been signaled to bring more refreshment, the company fell silent.

At length, their host sniffed, cleared his throat, and leaning forward once again addressed his audience. For by now he knew he had them where he wanted them—right in the palm of his puffy hand.

"Of course, it must go without saying, gentlemen, that the most desirable action that needs to take place as immediately as possible is the railroad—that is, the Northern Pacific—coming through Landers."

He paused, letting his eyes move to each face seated around the table. "I believe, gentlemen, I am seeing the eagerness, the questioning, the hope in your faces. And I know how much, how very much—let me say, by heaven, how damned much—each one of you wishes the Northern to include Landers in its march to the Western Sea."

He paused, reading them again: Calhoun Worth with his lips pursed, thinking how his bank could benefit; Pettiford, hard-bitten, wiry, all piss and vinegar, thinking about his goddam cows; Petersen and his store—the man would be in line for a fortune in trade; Wister of course, it couldn't fail to help his newspaper. As for Steiner, well the law had to be taken into account—but, to be sure, only up to a point.

It was Calhoun Worth who finally cleared his throat and said smoothly, "I expect there'll be a good bit of real estate involved with people wanting land along trackside, and for sure Landers will grow."

"Might even get a real good crack at becoming county seat," Petersen observed with a barely suppressed grin.

This brought a round of rough—though appreciative—laughter to the group.

"Might be a notion to get our hands on some of that land," said Worth. "Any of us interested in a good long-term return on the dollar."

Cecil Dunbellamy smiled quietly.

"What I wish to suggest, gentlemen, is that you form an official town council. Elect a leader such as a mayor, to officially head things, though the others of you who are here today would have a voice in decision making. The mayor would be your voice, so to say."

"Elect?" said Fifield Wister. "Who would run?"

"I suggest that it would be much simpler to *appoint* an acting mayor to start with," said Dunbellamy. "If you wait to have an election, you'll find too many people with their hand in the till. Appoint an acting mayor—not a mayor, but an acting mayor. That way, it is for the emergency, and provisional. Later, when things cool there can be an election held. Remember, it's always easier to drop an acting mayor, who by definition is temporary."

Petersen and the others turned their faces instantly toward the speaker even before he'd finished his sentence. "Emergency? But what emergency?" asked Calhoun Worth. "There isn't any emergency."

"That's right," said Hogarth Petersen. "What emergency?"

Cecil Dunbellamy was smiling as though he'd only just been waiting for the question. He looked like a tolerant parent or schoolmaster waiting for the young to exercise their limited intelligence, so that he could finally step in and tell it the way it really was.

"What emergency?" he repeated with a slight smile as though the questioner might have been funning him. "Why, the emergency that the council here will be engaged in muffling." He coughed almost apologetically into his fist. "After all, I don't see, for example, the Blackjack Gang—and others of that ilk as anything but dangerous to the present and future of Landers."

One or two faces seemed finally to get it—at least so Fifield Wister surmised as he looked around the table. But Hogarth Petersen still looked puzzled, and Tyson Pettiford frowned.

Cecil leaned his elbows on the edge of the table and leaned forward with his hands holding the sides of his head, the picture of inflexible patience as he waited for the meeting to transform into what he had so carefully been aiming for. Well, he almost sighed aloud, he had done his very best on this one by damn. Nobody could have expected more. He had done everything he could. For the fine art of his method lay in getting people to think that they themselves had thought of "it"— whatever "it" was—and thus not have to openly take on responsibility, yet still remain hooked.

"Emergency," Ed Steiner said presently. "Well, looks to me like I better get to work gettin' me some deputies."

He looked over at Cecil Dunbellamy, who returned his look, allowing an almost imperceptible smile at the corners of his mouth.

At a signal from Mr. Dunbellamy the waiter was called and arrived with a helper, both bearing more liquid refreshment, and some fine imported caviar. The caviar was an unfamiliar taste to almost the whole group—excepting Fifield

Wister, Calhoun Worth, and, of course, Cecil D. himself. But all, as it were, eagerly partook of the offering. Indeed, all had heard tell of Russian caviar, especially following the hunting trips of a number of European royalty; those parties never traveled more than a few feet from home minus the regally tasteful necessaries of civilized cuisine.

Shortly, Cecil rose to his feet. He had consumed almost no alcohol, although, veteran at such affairs as he was, he had been easily able to conceal the fact that he was drinking so much less than the others. But, after all, that was part of his trade, which he had started at an early age and he never tired of polishing what he had learned while at the same time addressing himself to what was new. His personal dictum was simple: to wit, that a man who lived by his wits had better learn every damn possible thing about his craft, his material, and especially about human beings that it was possible to learn. Thus, Cecil in his field was the eternal student, and happily so.

His present "promotion," to use his own word for it, was to be the crowning achievement of his well-planned career. He knew he was at the top and he delighted in his own dictum that there was always room at the top. A good deal such as the one presently at hand was worth everything.

And he smiled through the rich aroma of his fine imported Havana as he watched the reactions of those who were going to help

him—mostly unwittingly—on his field of con-
quest.

While Landers' End of the Journey Hotel was
famous for its "Prime Lodging," its cuisine, and
the quality of its service, O'Toole's Marvelous
Saloon and Dancing Establishment was definitely
not. O'Toole's was unabashedly a sound example
of the hell-on-wheels towns that were springing
up all through the West with the advent of the
transcontinental railway—even though Landers
itself was not a full-duty railroad town, but more
definitely oriented toward the cattle industry.

Even so, a spur had been laid to the town, over
which cattle cars chugged in and were loaded with
beeves bound for the slaughterhouses of Chicago,
the beef butcher of the world. But the great con-
tinental railway with its passengers and freight
had not yet reached that far west to really put
Landers on the map, in the sense that a railroad
and a booming town were married and in the
throes of spelling the big future for the Great
American West. It was toward this end that Cecil
Dunbellamy and his small army of adventurers,
which included bankers, lawyers, and politicians,
were now addressing themselves.

As a starter, Cecil Dunbellamy had sent his first
flatcars rumbling into the Landers station, which
was still in the process of being built. Every car
had been stacked high with knocked-down buildings, tents, roofs, dancehall floors, storefronts,
and wooden sidings.

In no time at all—or so it seemed to the dazed inhabitants—the End of the Journey Hotel was built and in business. It was a simple example of the railroad's march across the continent. It wasn't long before the knockdowns on those flatcars were all erected and the townsfolk—especially the leaders of the town—could see a fine example of what could be done to bring Landers into the limelight of the American West.

Cecil Dunbellamy and his associates to be sure were sensible enough to give only a taste to the inhabitants. For, as always, there was the question of money; that is to say, investment. And Cecil Dunbellamy was in Landers—as well as a number of other towns—to make this point quite clear.

Yet fine as the End of the Journey Hotel was, with its tasteful rooms and superior cuisine, Cecil Dunbellamy did not set up his headquarters in one of the attractive meeting rooms. He enjoyed the hotel as living quarters, and for the occasional meeting with special, more private business personnel. But for most of his business dealings with the Landers leaders he spent his time in one of the back rooms down the street at the ramshackle, though fully frequented, O'Toole's. Here, amidst dust, dirt, noise, and even drunken cavorting and not infrequent salacious entertainments, the refined gentleman with the face of a priest, the hands of a poker dealer, and the will and dry sense of humor of a professional gunfighter conducted much of his business.

At the moment, C.D.—as he mentally referred to himself—had wandered down the main street of Landers following his meeting with the "acting" town council at the End of the Journey, turning over in his mind what had transpired with his half dozen associates. It was a short walk, and in less than fifteen minutes he had reached his "second headquarters."

As he pushed through the bat-wing doors at O'Toole's, he was instantly aware of the temper of the big room. The place was crowded, as usual, no matter the hour, and it was noisy. There was the inevitable line of chairs tilted against the back wall, all of them occupied, and, of course, the thick congress of drinkers at the bar, with foot on brass rail and elbows on the long mahogany, which ran the width of the big room. The room looked even bigger and busier thanks to the huge mirror behind the bar, doubling everything.

His eye immediately caught the group standing to his left. One of the three was speaking, nobody later remembering which one it had been—nor did it matter—for the pistol shot that rang out so suddenly brought the room into that immediate silence that results from sudden violence.

One shot. A six-gun. And the thump of a heavy body hitting the floor. Later, somebody put it that the silence could have been carved real fine with a skinning knife.

But Cecil Dunbellamy, along with others, saw that the body on the floor was not dead. Nor was it there as the result of lead, but rather from the fist of the brute standing over him.

"Get up! Get on your feet, you little sonofabitch and haul ass out of Landers and I mean right now!"

The man on the floor was struggling, slowly working to his feet. Blood flowed from his nose and his cheekbone was already swelling. He was just halfway erect when the big man in the black shirt and wide black Stetson hat smashed him in the side of the neck. The victim fell like a sack of grain to the floor and lay still.

"Sonofabitch! I told you to git yer ass outta town. Didn't you hear me, fer Chrissakes!"

"C'mon, Killigan. He's had enough." The man speaking was standing behind the bar. He was also a big man, and muscular. And he was clearly unafraid of the man he called Killigan.

"Felix, you keep yer fuckin' mouth shut!"

"Killigan . . ."

"Or I'll shut it for you!"

"Killigan, have a drink. On the house, lad. But calm down."

But those words were hardly out of the bartender's mouth before the man named Killigan, as somebody later described it "quicker'n a cat can lick his own ass, by God he reached down to the chair near him, picked up a coiled lariat rope an' snapped the end with the leather thong right into Pat Callaghan's face."

The movement was so totally unexpected that the entire room was stunned into graveside silence, while the bartender let out a scream of pain and clutched at his savaged face.

Killigan, grinning in victory, wheeled on the room, focusing on Harold, Stacey, and Lennie. "Get him outta here," he snapped. And his head turned swiftly to the swinging doors as a man walked in, duly armed with a six-gun at his hip, and with a striking alertness in his easy movement. On the instant, seeing the interesting tableau before him he stopped, and brought his hands slowly to his gunbelt, where he now hooked his thumbs. Thus, Clint Adams and Bowdrie Killigan faced each other.

Cecil Dunbellamy instantly caught the drama and, fully aware of his own excitement, pushed his way forward for a better view.

Fifield Wister, just recently arrived on the scene, was to describe it later on the front page in his rich frontier prose: "The twain faced each other, a first meeting between the man known under the colorful sobriquet of 'The Gunsmith,' and the giant known as 'The Man from North of Hell.' They sized each other up, and seemed to dismiss each other. But that is hardly to be believed. Gunfighters are invariably jealous of their reputations, and there couldn't have been a man in that crowded room who wasn't aware of the violent possibilities of such a pregnant encounter."

But Bowdrie Killigan was a man filled with surprises. No one ever really knew where they were with such a man. Right now he was bent almost double roaring with laughter; slapping his thigh with one hand, bringing his other arm down like a scythe as he pumped out his great cackling, roaring guffaws. The entire saloon, stunned into silence, stared at him.

The community was used to these outbursts, or at any rate appeared to be. The men stood there without reacting, at any rate externally. This was mostly because they had learned from experience that it could be dangerous to react to Bowdrie Killigan. A man could be sure that whatever he did—be it laughing with him or simply just nodding agreement with some outrageous behavior—it would be wrong. The citizenry had learned this the hard way. As a number of broken bones, sprained wrists and shoulders, sore crotches from receiving a swift kick, and other veteran body wounds could bear testimony. With Mr. Killigan a man never knew which way to go. Even just standing there doing nothing, not even looking at him and his crazy antics—even this neutral action could bring sudden and massive retaliation.

Now, suddenly, the man who had commanded the total attention of the room stopped. He stood absolutely still, his big eyes glowing, his chest heaving somewhat, but with no other evident movement. It was the suddenness of Mr. Killigan's changes that got to people. It was the unexpected mixed with the violent that was feared. Not a man in Landers would ever forget how Bowdrie Killigan had once pistol-whipped a man for yawning in his presence.

Suddenly Cecil Dunbellamy was aware—in a way that was rare for him—that he was standing at the edge of the crowded room rooted to the spot. It seemed that here right in front of his eyes was the excitement which exceeded even his stripping a poker game, rolling endless sevens, or capping a deal. As good as, maybe better than, the best bedroom tussles he'd had with Consuelo, his utterly lascivious companion, or even some others he'd known through the years. And yet, born gambler that he was, something in him insisted he remain calm, cool, collected.

By God, he was telling himself, by God he couldn't have asked for better. Killigan and Adams, the Gunsmith. Now he could see, he could answer some of the questions that had been building in his mind for a good while. Who was the better? He already had Killigan on his payroll and his plan to nab Adams was surely unfolding. He was indeed experiencing the highest satisfaction in seeing right before his eyes how his careful plan to induce the man known as the Gunsmith to come to Landers was working.

It had not been easy. Not at all easy setting up Wayne Behrens down in Foster's Gap with a managed investigation that drew his interest into Landers, then getting him shot, and gambling— yes gambling—on Behrens asking Adams to take his place. By damn! A real stroke of luck! Everything was coming his way. Well, he had earned it. By God, he had earned it, and he deserved it. In spades.

Meanwhile, he was actively watching the two men in the center of the big room where the big

space around them had gotten bigger as some
people had left the premises.

Cecil smiled to himself. He'd sent the marshal
on a fool's errand up to Fort Larrabee, to make
sure he was out of the way when he dealt with
the pair he was now watching. For the confronta-
tion that was now developing before the whole of
O'Toole's Saloon was working exactly to his satisfaction. Not for nothing had he pumped Killigan
full of bravura about being "Top Gun," and a
whole lot better, tougher, and faster than that
one they called the Gunsmith. Killigan had eat-
en it up.

Now, watching the scene unfolding in O'Toole's
big barroom, C.D. was almost laughing out loud
at the excitement he had authored so carefully
and, yes, skillfully. Everything in him seemed to
be hammering now as he felt the climax of the
drama reaching its final moment.

As Fifield Wister wrote it later in *The Landers
Bugle*, "Nobody dropped a pin because nobody
moved even an eyelid. But if a pin had dropped,
then it surely would have been heard!"

"Well, what kin I do for you . . ." Bowdrie
Killigan started to say.

"Nothing."

The single word came like a knife, cutting the
big man off at the pockets. All noticed there was
not a trace of fear or anger, not even the slightest
concern, in the Gunsmith's tone of voice. He simply stood where he was, not at all adopting any
sort of gunfighter stance. He might have been
discussing the time of day.

"Nothing!" barked the Man from North of Hell. "Well, by God, that is for sure a piss-poor answer . . . ! He glared at the man facing him, hard and tight with building anger, while the man known as The Gunsmith, by no means inattentive, simply remained.

Silence had descended as the two faced each other. Both Fifield Wister and Cecil Dunbellamy noted that they could hear the breathing of the crowd.

Then Bowdrie Killigan's face creased into sudden mirth. He chuckled. He looked around the room.

"Mister, I see you be a man of few words," he said.

"And I use them few damn seldom," the Gunsmith replied, remembering an old-timer who from time to time offered the same when questioned. But neither Clint Adams' face nor his stance had lost its attention. As every man in the room could see, he was ready. He kept his eyes firmly on those of the man facing him, but was also well aware of Killigan's hands, his feet, everything about him, especially his atmosphere.

It was a long moment for some of the spectators, and for a good many it was the longest they'd ever experienced.

Finally, Bowdrie Killigan said, "Buy you a drink, mister."

Clint Adams said nothing. For another second or two he kept his eyes on the big man standing there with his back to the bar. Then he turned and without a backward look walked quietly out of the room, the crowd parting to give him passage.

The Gunsmith did not look back, his step didn't hesitate, and Cecil Dunbellamy could detect not the slightest tightening in his shoulders, back, or any unevenness in his measured gait.

The bat-wing doors slapped shut as the man who had faced down Bowdrie Killigan departed the scene.

For a moment the silence lengthened. Then somebody sneezed. And someone else started to say something which couldn't be heard, but stopped.

Big Bowdrie Killigan continued to stand where he was with his thick thumbs hooked into his gunbelt. Fifield Wister was wondering how he could leave without attracting the attention of Mr. Killigan. But the crowded room had indeed started to stir a little, each man careful not to make any larger or noisier movement than anyone else.

And then suddenly Killigan spoke. His big red face was twisted into what could have been a smile, his words were easy, and yet nobody in the room missed what their real meaning amounted to.

" 'Pears that feller what's called Gunsmith or whatever, he looks to be likin' our community here. I am guessin' he'd maybe favor takin' up permanent residence."

Someone in the crowd started to laugh, but stopped. Someone else coughed. There was a muted shuffling of feet. Big Bowdrie Killigan remained where he was, staring just above the heads of the gathering.

Fifield Wister found that he had been holding his breath, and was already wondering what, if anything, he could write of the scene that had just transpired.

Cecil Dunbellamy couldn't have been more pleased with the little play that had just been enacted. But he took note of how his breathing was changed, how—by damn—he himself was changed.

Suddenly Killigan stepped up to the bar. Reaching into his trouser pocket he pulled out money and slapped it onto the mahogany.

"Boys, the drinks are on me! Drink up. We got somethin' good to celebrate seein' as how we got shut of that Gunsmith feller in jig-time!"

Watching the scene of Killigan attempting to redeem himself, Cecil almost grinned. He had chosen well, very well. Now he had the two elements that could really power what he had in mind for his next step.

FIVE

"Feller come by around the middle of the fore-noon," the old hostler said.

"You're saying he was looking for myself." The Gunsmith had taken out a wooden match and, slipping one end between his teeth, began chewing on it.

"More like lookin' for the black," the hostler said, squinting one eye as he canted his head toward Clint.

"This forenoon."

The old boy, parsimonious with his words, nodded.

"Tall, skinny? Big nose, huh?"

"I'd say about your size,'cepting' a bit hefty in the belly."

"What did he do?" Clint asked, feeling anger rise in him at the thought of somebody messing with Duke.

"Pretended he was looking to bring his hoss down from the hitch rail uptown. Figurin' to stay the night like."

"So?"

"So he wanted a look at the place. An' he seen the black there and went over and took a closer look." The oldster sniffed, then spat eloquently at a pile of fresh horse manure in the corral where they were standing right outside the livery. " 'Nice piece of hossflesh,' he says, like keepin' his eye on me."

"Uh-huh." Clint continued to chew the end of the match.

"Said as how he hadn't seen such a hoss in this good while, not since up in Deadwood."

"Deadwood, huh?"

"That is what he said. Asked who owned it."

"You told him?"

"I told him nothin'. Didn't you tell me to keep an eye on that hoss whilst here in the livery? Well, goddammit, that is what I been doin'. That was a dumb question, mister."

"Just makin' certain," the Gunsmith said equably, his face absolutely still. He squinted at the sun. "You reckon he is figurin' something, do you?"

"More'n likely, I'd wager."

"Huh." Clint Adams was looking down at the toe of his boot.

"Figure it'd be better you took yer hoss someplace else, mister. I don't want that kind of trouble."

"Tell me what he looked like."

"Like I already told. Chunky, cast in his left eye, an' he had big hands."

The description meant nothing to Clint Adams. He'd been thinking it might have been one of the three who had tried to bushwhack him.

"You are sure he was fixin' to mess with my horse?"

"I am not sure, mister. I just thought his questions was interestin'." He spat. "You told me to watch for anything or any person messing around."

"That's what I know," the Gunsmith said. "Just trying to make sure we don't go off half-cocked on a false alarm."

"We!?"

"I am hiring you to help me," Clint said. "Which is what you're supposed to be doin' as concerns my horse in the first place."

"Mister, I am a old man, beat up from too much—"

"From too much boozing," the Gunsmith said, without a trace of pity in his voice. "Now you can do something good for a change, more than just sitting around bullshitting and bitching about how tough you've got it." Reaching into his pocket he took out money. "You'll get paid. What kind of a weapon you got there?"

"Got my old Remington .50 carbine, but while she ain't been used in real long I got her oiled and the action ain't bad."

Clint grinned at him. "Now that's more like it, mister."

"Huh?"

"I am saying I knew you had it in you to help me."

He watched the hostler's big Adam's apple pump up and down a couple of times.

"Mister, after what I heard you done to Bowdrie Killigan in O'Toole's I ain't about to argue different with you. Just tell me what you want done."

It didn't take the Gunsmith long to figure it out. He still wasn't sure whether or not the old hostler was in on it, but it was clear that the move in the direction of Duke had been a feint. Clearly, no purpose would be served in injuring somebody's horse no matter how much its owner valued it. On the other hand, there would be apparent value in threatening such an action. Clint Adams could speculate on the fact that someone was trying to corral him. Indeed, he could feel the almost barely visible connection between the shooting of Wayne Behrens, the three toughs on the trail who had attacked him, and the strange setup with the big man named Killigan. Not to forget the presence of Melanie, the delightful bedfriend who had been set up in his hotel room.

But to what purpose? And who was on his trail? He could feel the presence of someone, or even more than one, watching his moves. Melanie had been the first. Killigan the second. Maybe there had even been somebody back at Foster's Gap. Yes, now reflecting on it as he ate breakfast at the Find It Cafe down Main Street near the stock pens, he was pretty sure the story had started back with Wayne Behrens. Somebody—whoever had been behind the shooting of Wayne—was onto him. The question was why had somebody dry-gulched Behrens? What had Wayne found, or stumbled on? Or to whom or what had he gotten so close that he would be threatened, and actually shot up? Had he, Clint Adams, been set up for a killing? Or was someone just figuring to frighten him off because he was getting too close to something—something maybe pretty big? And Clint was feeling more and more certain that there was indeed something very big being cooked. And then too, maybe somebody had been trying to get to himself, and Wayne Behrens actually had been a pawn. Yes, maybe he himself was the principal target.

With these questions in his mind he wasn't at all surprised to see the room clerk avoiding him. The moment Clint walked into the lobby, the old boy ducked right out from behind his desk and was gone, walking fast and tight, as though he had to make it to the outhouse and fast.

Clint stepped behind the desk, took his key, and then started up the stairs.

On the landing he stepped back into the hall so that he couldn't be seen by the clerk or by anyone on the floor below. As he'd figured the old boy was back almost instantly. So he had indeed wanted to avoid him. The Gunsmith had a sudden notion to get on back down the stairs and quiz the old man, but changed his mind. The clerk was obviously too frightened to make much sense. And it was pretty obvious that he had a visitor.

He was just about to put his key in the lock when he heard the movement inside, and another behind him on the stairs.

He reacted swiftly with the realization that he was trapped. He drew his gun, dropped to his knee as he spun to face the man behind him, and fired. Not even waiting for the attacker to fall he spun to his left and shot a man who had come out of one of the rooms down the hall with his six-gun kicking. The Gunsmith felt something tug at his sleeve, but he knew he wasn't hit.

He turned again, kicked the door of his room open and jumped to one side. He could hear a thump and a crash in the street outside and in the next moment he was inside his room and looking at the open window where the third attacker had obviously jumped.

Three of them! Well, he felt good as he reloaded the Colt. For like many men—if not all—who relied on their guns, the Gunsmith was always aware of the fact that one day he could grow older and slower, with the reflexes and keeness of sense that he relied on so thoroughly possibly weakened. It was sure damn good to know he was still able.

Stepping quickly to the broken window frame he looked down into the street, actually an alley elbow. Yes, there he was hobbling away, but he had no desire to shoot the would-be killer like that. It was not his way.

Coming back into the room, he instantly caught the step outside in the hall and moved quickly to the side of the door which he had left open in his fast move to the window.

The visitor came slowly down the hall, making no attempt to be quiet. In the next moment a voice called out, "Mr. Adams? Are you in?" And this was accompanied by a few knocks on the open door.

Clint did not recognize the voice, but noted that it was obviously a man's.

"You can come in and find out, if you've a mind to," said the Gunsmith, with his hand not far at all from his still holstered sixgun.

The figure who entered brought to his mind the word *dude*, then *tenderfoot*, then a few other words like banker, business, and finally railroad.

"I am Cecil Dunbellamy," the visitor said. "Might I come in?"

Clint Adams thought the accent might be partly English. Certainly it was no homegrown Wyoming voice, choice of words, appearance, and especially attitude and general bearing that greeted him.

"What can I do for you, mister?" he asked. He let his hand drop away from his holstered gun slowly; but obviously, expecting the visitor to understand what could have happened, could still happen.

"Well, er . . ." The pause came, it seemed intentionally to Clint Adams. The man was certainly unruffled, even though he must have realized he could have been hurt coming in at such a moment. And he must have known what had taken place, for the Gunsmith would have bet the works that the man standing there with a tentative smile on his face, appraising him with those cold, gambler eyes, was no dude, no easy mark, no fool.

Then the Gunsmith took a gamble. "Your associate left pretty quick, if it's him you're looking for, mister. By the window, and he was damn lucky I let him get away."

"And why did you let him get away?" Cecil Dunbellamy asked.

"On account of I like to look at the man I'm shooting." Clint let a wry smile touch his eyes, the corners of his mouth. "Reckon you're of a different school, aren't you?"

Cecil Dunbellamy's smile was almost a grin of pleasure as he took another step into the room. "Might I shut the door and sit down? Perhaps there on the edge of the bed? I wanted to talk to you."

Clint Adams said nothing. He simply stood there with his eyes on his visitor, watching how the man met his lack of response. Cecil Dunbellamy let his smile broaden.

"I'll bet you're quite a poker player, Mr. Adams. I think I'd like to deal a hand or two with you some time."

"Looks to me like you're doing that right now," said Clint Adams quietly. "Tell me what you want." And he added, "You could have spoken to me in the saloon. Why didn't you?"

And he caught the surprise in the other man's face.

"You're just the man I'm looking for, Mr. Adams."

"My gun is not for hire, mister. I only use it against trash like the kind you sent."

"I'm not talking about your gun, Adams, but your brain. I admire the way you take charge, the way you handled Killigan, the big loudmouth. I need a man—a real man. Not a bully or show-off. I didn't send those men to kill you, but I needed to test you. I wanted to see if you were all that I'd heard." He grinned. "And you are."

The Gunsmith had reached over with his foot and pushed the door shut. Then, reaching for the room's only chair, he turned it so that its back was facing his visitor, and sat down. He nodded toward the bed. "You can sit there."

"Obliged," Cecil Dunbellamy said, and there was a tight little smile in his eyes and at his mouth.

A beat followed as the visitor settled himself. Reaching to his pocket he took out a cigar, offering it.

"Smoke?"

Clint simply shook his head very slightly. "This room doesn't smell all that good already," he declared. "A cigar isn't going to help."

"Right." And a little chuckle bounced out of Dunbellamy's mouth as he returned the cigar to his pocket and put his hands down beside him on the edge of the bed.

Clint Adams waited.

Cecil Dunbellamy pursed his lips.

"It's interesting having your company, mister, but I don't have all that much time. So tell your business."

His visitor smiled quickly, cleared his throat, and said, "I understand you are looking for the men who shot Wayne Behrens, the Federal Marshal who was, I believe, investigating something or other in or around Landers. Am I correct here?"

Clint nodded, and said nothing.

"I believe I might be able to help you."

"Shoot."

"Behrens was investigating the Blackjack gang. At least, that's what I've heard."

"You a part of that gang?" the Gunsmith asked, and his face was pure innocence.

"Mr. Adams, that is not funny. No. I am connected with the Northern Pacific Railroad. I guess you might call me a sort of advance agent. You know of the competition between the Northern Pacific and the Union Transcontinental; to be first to span this continent."

"By now with all the bullshit that's been filling the fresh air I'd be deaf, dumb, and blind if I didn't."

Cecil Dunbellamy pursed his lips, as though trying to decide which way to go with what he had in mind.

Suddenly he leaned forward, his elbows on his knees, his fingertips together, while an earnest wrinkling appeared in his forehead.

"But there are certain elements, certain people who are trying to spoil our work with the Northern Pacific, and I believe—although I do not know for certain—that Wayne Behrens was investigating that. In other words, Behrens was working quietly—you could say secretly—for us, for the N.P." He paused. Then, cocking an eye at his host. "I don't know how much of this you already know. I only know that you and Wayne Behrens were friends. And while I don't know how close that friendship was, I can only guess that with a man of your quality it would not be something trivial. In a word, I have been gambling on the point that Behrens might very well have confided in you on certain matters."

"Certain matters concerning what?" Clint Adams asked.

"Concerning the railroad. That is to say, the activities of those who were clearly trying to hinder the N.P. Notably—at any rate we suspect—the Blackjack gang."

"How can that gang stop a railroad?" Clint asked, though he knew very well what his visitor was getting at. "I mean, a gang can pull some holdups, pretty big ones, on existing trains, but how would they stop a line from getting built?"

"Blackmail."

"You mean, they would frighten off anyone who might want the railroad to go through a different part of the country than they wanted."

"That's it."

"So who do you think dry-gulched Wayne Behrens?"

"I don't know. But I suspect the Blackjack gang."

"Butch Mulligan still whipsawing that outfit?"

"I don't know. Adams, I should explain to you that I am in the executive part of the N.P. And I've been sent out here to see how much the towns involved would wish for the N.P. to include them in their stops."

"I do understand that, Dunbellamy. And I understand very well how the, well, rival railroad would prefer the towns in mind to choose their service." His voice was as innocent as a sweet song, and he cautioned himself to go carefully. "In other words, we're talking real estate,

land values, and eventually votes and politics,"
Clint said.

"Of course. I suppose that's so." Letting his
voice drift away into innocent speculation, Cecil
was beginning to find Clint Adams not at all an
easy nut to crack.

The Gunsmith reached into his shirt pocket
and drew out a sack of Bull Durham and his cigarette papers. Both he and his visitor remembered
clearly his earlier objection to cigar smoke.

Well, Dunbellamy reflected, cigar smoke was
indeed stronger than the built cigarette. But he
knew very well, too, that the man seated in front
of him was telling him something very clear: to
wit, that he was nobody to be whipsawed. Of
course, Cecil consoled himself with the knowledge that he had known that already.

Quietly, letting the silence handle itself as it
slipped into the room now, Clint Adams built his
smoke while his visitor watched.

It was just as Clint struck the wooden lucifer
and lighted up that Cecil decided it was time for
him to come to his main point. At the same time
that he reached this decision he found his host's
eyes directly on him. And all at once he felt the
situation was getting his goat and not going just
the way he had wanted, and this irritated him
even more. At the same time, Cecil Dunbellamy
was a professional in his chosen, self-created field
and so nothing actually got out of his hand. In
fact, he began to feel a special elation at having
found exactly the man he wanted for what he had
in mind.

"I don't want to take any more of your time, Adams. I want to get to the point of my visit. Which is to invite you to join my enterprise . . . uh . . . in a certain capacity—"

"You want to hire my gun. I already told you no." And he stood up.

"I don't quite mean that the way it may have sounded to you, Adams. Do let me explain."

"No. I'm busy now," And he was standing, sweeping the chair out from under him. Then, crossing to the door, he opened it.

His visitor, slightly flushed in the face, was also standing. By now he had his cigar in his hand, though he did not light it.

But Cecil Dunbellamy had no intention of letting it go just like that.

"I wish you would give it more thought," he said pleasantly.

The Gunsmith said nothing.

They were standing right in the doorway now.

"The play would be . . . well, something very satisfying, I assure you. You would have a completely free hand. And in spite of what you appear to be thinking, it would have nothing to do with your . . ." He dropped his eyes pointedly to the belt and holstered gun that the Gunsmith was wearing. "With law enforcement. I have plenty of people for that. Indeed, a solid cadre of lawmen, dedicated to their work. Your position would be more—you might say more on the planning end, dealing with the overall picture; the how, why, and where of a specific operation or event. Look . . ." He suddenly stopped and spread his little hands, palms up.

"Look, try it. Give it a try. You can always quit. Adams, the West needs the best railroad it can get. The entire country needs the kind of railroad it deserves. It's my job to see the people get what they need and, yes, want."

The Gunsmith stood there with his eyes right on the man who had made his play. It was all there; Clint read it clearly. It could not have been said better. And the whole affair began to fit just like a puzzle where the pieces suddenly and unaccountably came to hand. What Dunbellamy was offering in his outline sketch was simply the threat that he, Clint Adams, would not interfere, would not pursue the search for whoever had shot and killed Wayne Behrens. For, clearly, Dunbellamy's operation was running smoothly; it had been at any rate, until Wayne Behrens had started to dig into it. It was as plain as the famous old pikestaff that there was plenty of hanky-panky afoot, and Wayne had found it. Now, of course, if Dunbellamy could point to the Gunsmith being on his side—in fact, working for him—he'd have more than a leg up with the Northern and the N.P. would be smelling like an angel.

Clint Adams didn't return the nod that Cecil Dunbellamy gave as he turned and started back down the corridor. At the head of the stairs he looked back, smiled—but clearly without mirth or goodwill—and disappeared down to the lobby.

Clint Adams returned to his room. He knew that now Dunbellamy and the men who were working with him would go all out to make good use of the Gunsmith and his reputation.

He lay down on the bed wondering idly for a moment whether Dunbellamy would go for threat or bribe. Both if necessary, of course. But though it was an idle question, only at the edge of his mind, he knew that it was just a matter of time before he found out what Dubellamy's next move would be.

He took off his hat and boots, then lay there on his back with his hands together behind his head. It was an old brass-poster bed and it rang out whenever he moved, almost when he even breathed; as he considered what the alternatives were.

Short of an out-and-out bushwhacking or cold-blooded murder, there wasn't much they could do. He wasn't especially vulnerable, having no family or special friends, or . . .

And suddenly he sat up in bed and swung his feet to the floor, first putting on his hat—like any real cowhand—then pulling on his boots.

Five minutes later he was on his way down to the livery.

SIX

"Hear the latest?" The old hostler had that look in his craggy face that spelled hard news.

But the Gunsmith was ready. "Maybe. Depends how much latest you're talkin' about."

"Early yestiddy morning a bunch of owlhooters hit the Double Bar Z on the South Fork and run off about thirty head of beeves. Got clean away, they did. Old man Pettiford's fit to be tied, and he's got his men out hell-for-leatherin' all the way up to Squaw Pass."

"Huh." The Gunsmith sniffed and reached to his shirt pocket, pulling out the makings. "How's Duke is what I come to see you about. He looks good, but I am thinking of moving him."

"He's doin' fine. Ain't been nobody about askin' after his health an' like that."

"Good enough."

"Hear about the doin's at Hogarth Petersen's?"

"Heard some noise early this morning, but figgered it was some of the boys celebrating a

85

bit previous to the Fourth."

"Those boys was celebratin' by robbing Petersen deaf, dumb, an' blind. And gettin' plumb away with it."

Clint Adams looked at the horizon, squinting against the early morning sunlight.

"What you figger?" the hostler asked.

"I figger what you figger."

"The two is connected."

Clint nodded. "There'll be more. And," he added. "There'll for sure be a posse riding out."

"That's the size of it," the old man said. "Somebody's aimin' to buffalo this town, but I guess I am 'bout the only human here who sees it that way." And he squinted at Clint Adams, as he scratched his behind. " 'Ceptin' yerself, I reckon,"

"You are figuring that it smells."

"I am. But I am a voice of one, which I am keeping quiet."

"Tell me something," the Gunsmith said.

"Shoot."

"Tell me why you're telling me all this."

The hostler's shock filled his face and he even took a small step toward the Gunsmith, as though his surprise was too much for him. "I don't get you, mister."

"You get me," snapped Clint. "You get me and now you tell me who put you up to telling me."

"Why—why no one. No one told me nothin'! An' that's the God's honest truth! I swear it, mister."

"Bullshit," said Clint Adams and he walked into

the livery to see his horse again.

Duke was standing quietly in his stall. He looked good and it was clear that he was being well taken care of.

"Been really handling that hoss of yours, mister." The old boy came up softly, though with heavy breathing, sucking his gums a bit, and now and again scratching at various parts of his aged body. "Ain't been nobody about payin' any mind to your hoss, and that's the God's honest . . ."

Clint just stood there staring at him, as he debated whether or not the old-timer was telling the truth.

"Good enough then," he said finally, satisfied. "I think you're telling me straight. Fact, I believe they'll be leaving my horse be."

"Glad to hear it."

"So am I." And he could see it was so. If Cecil Dunbellamy had any sense at all, the last thing he would do would be to try anything with Duke.

The Gunsmith also knew that it wouldn't be because of any humanitarian feelings on the part of Mr. Dunbellamy, but rather simple good sense. Except it might not be Cecil Dunbellamy who might try something.

"So what else is happening?" he asked as the old hostler stood there scratching himself and sniffing.

"Sheriff's gettin' up a posse to go after the buggers. And 'sides that, I hear they're running in a trainload of them immy-grants on that train spur, or whatever the hell it calls it."

"Spur is right," Clint said. "What do you reck-on all those people are going to do here around Landers?"

"I'll be askin' you the same, mister."

"I see." Clint looked across at Duke, then turned, and without saying any more, he started out of the barn. The old man fell in beside him.

Now they stood in the round horse corral. The old man's name was Quince but, as he'd told the Gunsmith, "They useter call me Snake River Quince in the old days, but now it's just Quince. Shorter." He paused, standing close to his companion when they heard the gunshots, followed by the galloping sound of maybe four or five horses, shouts, and then all was still.

"Shit," said the old man. "Shit take it."

"When are the immigrants due?" Clint asked.

"Reckon any day now. Leastways from what I hear."

"Would you say the boys have been getting more feisty?"

"You mean like them just now?"

"I do."

The old man squinted, almost closing one eye, and with the other half closed suddenly let fly a thick brown and yellow stream of chewing tobac-co and saliva.

After a moment Quince said, "Wonder what you might be studyin' all this time, mister. Like you wuz thinkin' real hard about somethin, huh."

Clint Adams was looking at the sky, where the evening was just getting ready to slip in. He had sometimes wondered just when light became dark, and in the morning dark became light. At what precise point was day turned into night? Well, it didn't matter, he was thinking now. What counted was the way things had changed, what they were turning into, and how and why.

Now again they heard the drumming of galloping horses, each knowing of course what that meant. Horses were not allowed to gallop in the dirt streets of any western town of any size, and certainly not in Landers. Yet, here it had happened two–three times in the short while that Clint Adams had been with the old man. The Gunsmith did not see this as anything but a bad sign.

A faint star suddenly seemed to appear near the horizon and Clint was glad to see it. Twilight was always the best time of day for him.

"What you thinking?" the old man asked him suddenly.

" 'Bout the weather mostly. Looks like it might be fixin' for some rain come tomorrow."

"I was talkin' about what's been happenin', and what it seems like most people don't have no notion of it."

The suspicion of a grin came into Clint Adams' face. "Well, I was thinking about that," he said. "Some anyways."

"So what was you thinkin' about?" the oldster persisted.

"I was . . . well, I guess I was thinkin' about how a man can't count on something happening the way he might've thought it would in the first place."

• • •

Engineer Ham Grover started as he heard the sharp explosion that sounded so much like the crack of a rifle. His train was chugging along through Squaw Teat Canyon where the close rock walls made wild echoes, and he had fixed the engine cab tight against a night storm.

He strained to see better. His headlight was making a shimmery halo in the rain in front of his train. He opened a window, and immediately took the storm full in his face. He heard another loud crack, and then he saw a red spot in the halo.

"It's got to be trouble!" he shouted to Mulligan, his fireman. And he suddenly realized with a chill racing through him that the explosions had been rail torpedoes. Instantly, he was braking down as fast as he could. The warning flare was only yards ahead. A wash-out, likely. Or maybe . . .

He leaned way out of his cab, squinting for better vision, as the train stopped short. Without realizing it, he had instinctively reached beside his cab seat for his handgun.

"That'll be it!" a voice shouted from the darkness surrounding them. "Hit the sky! Hands up Grover! And by God, you too, Mulligan!"

Ham Grover couldn't see anybody out there, but in sudden anger, which had come to the boil, he shot at the voice.

In return he received a fusillade. He collapsed, his anger leaving him, along with everything else, as he slumped and hung limply out the window of the train he had tried so stoutly to defend.

Meanwhile, Mulligan was crouching near the firebox until a man with a mask climbed, cursing, into the cab.

But by now much was happening in the express car which was immediately behind the engine. Expressman and guard both knew they were carrying a large shipment of money. And they had heard the shouting. The guard, a man still in his youth, drew his handgun and ran to the little glass window of the car to peer out. Two shots and he twisted around on himself and fell, stone dead.

The expressman had the presence of mind to realize that it would be total folly to offer further resistance. Yet he did rush to the doors and locked them. Then swiftly he took a few leather bags from the safe. There were a good many more, but he couldn't handle them all. The bags were heavy. Frantically he looked about for a hiding place. At one end of the car was a pot-bellied stove with a fire in it. He opened the door and crammed the bags in, figuring no doubt, even if gold melts, it is still gold. He kicked the stove door shut.

The bandits didn't hesitate. When they discovered the express door locked they planted a stick of dynamite under the car and fired it.

The explosion was enormous, tearing away one whole side of the car. A brace of armed, masked men instantly climbed aboard. The expressman was crouching behind a desk at the far end of the car, miraculously unhurt.

"Get over there and open that safe!" snapped one of the outlaws.

The sensible man obeyed. In less than a half dozen minutes the two highwaymen had passed out leather bags. Then, warning the expressman not to make any move, they mounted their waiting horses and disappeared into the stormy night.

Sheriff Ed Steiner reached the scene two hours later, still foggy from his deep sleep, aided by a few too many drinks the evening before. But when he realized the extent of the robbery he woke up pretty fast. Total money in the shipment was $50,000, but there was the gold that had been melted in the stove, and this amount came to about $10,000, which was unharmed. The bandits had gotten away with $40,000, plus two murders and the wrecked express car, making it one of the worst crimes ever in the entire Wyoming area. And it was clear to the sheriff that the robbery was the work of men who were obviously experienced as well as fearless. They were also lucky— because of the rain their tracks would be washed well away.

Stumped, at any rate for the moment, Sheriff Ed Steiner and his men withdrew to Landers to await a break in the weather. But reporting to Cecil Dunbellamy threw a different light on the subject.

"Sheriff, I suggest—I strongly suggest—that you get Clint Adams on the job. I know you're short-handed and I know how hard it is to get deputies, especially good ones. But this is the third holdup in the past six weeks, and that's just the railroad!

As you know, we've also had a rash of stage robberies, and even the number of travelers getting robbed has increased."

"Mr. Dunbellamy, I got to get some help."

"That is precisely what I have just been telling you."

"Will you speak to Adams then?" Steiner asked.

"I want you to speak to him, Sheriff. It will be much better coming directly from the law, so to say. The beleaguered law officer is asking for help." He held up his hand, feeling the objection springing into the lawman's throat.

"I, of course, could get Adams to help you. He's a decent man, and would certainly do what I ask. But this is more a civic business that's the problem."

"It's the railroad," Steiner pointed out.

"Quite. Indeed it is the railroad, but it is the people's money. That money was going to the bank and would be paying the Northern Pacific for the new spur that would include Landers in their schedule. Losing it, we not only injure the people involved, but we risk losing the spur as well. Not to mention the passenger train service, and what it would do for the town. Landers—you know this as well as I do—Landers needs and really must have the Northern Pacific, and that money is vital. I'd even hazard the guess that whoever pulled that job was working for the Union Transcontinental."

His words sobered the atmosphere in a flash. The sheriff saw the sense of it. But that didn't mean he liked it. He had seen Clint Adams in action with Killigan, and he had no wish to mess with such a man.

Cecil Dunbellamy was smiling, sizing his man accurately. "He has his heart and his guts in the right place, Sheriff. Clint Adams will help you. Anyway, he wouldn't want to run the risk of having the whole town of Landers turn against him for refusing us help in our hour of need. Now, would he?"

And his warmest smile stroked the sheriff of Landers all the way through. Especially when Dunbellamy added, "With yourself and Adams on the job—yourself naturally in charge—you cannot fail. Landers needs a champion in its difficulty. And without that money, if those men get away with it, Landers is dead." He put his arm around the other man's shoulders. "I have every confidence in you, Sheriff. Ed," he added.

He stood in the middle of the room he was using for an office, and listened to the sheriff's footsteps fading down the corridor outside.

Cecil remained where he was. He was thinking. He took out his watch and looked at the time, but even before a thought could form in his brain, there came a light tapping at the other door.

He crossed swiftly, saying "Come in," as he unlocked the door and opened it.

"My dear, you are precisely on time, but I must ask you to wait just a few minutes longer. I'm done with my main business, but there is just one more thing I have to take care of. It won't take five minutes." And there came a knock on

the other door, the one through which Sheriff Ed
Steiner had departed.

The girl smiled. "I can't bear to wait, C.D., but
I will. Please hurry!" And she was in his arms,
spreading her legs so he could push his erection
between them.

"I can't wait either," he said. "I won't be long."

And the knock came again.

"Sometimes a little waiting helps it more," she
said, smiling as she stood there looking at his
mouth.

"Give me five minutes," he said. She winked,
licking her lips. "Three," he said as he held the
door for her.

And now when the knock came for the third
time he crossed the room swiftly and opened the
door.

"Thought you might of got caught up someplace," said Bowdrie Killigan as he stomped into
the room and Cecil closed the door behind him.

"Things have been piling up," Dunbellamy said,
and then admonished himself instantly for sound-
ing apologetic.

"What did you want to see me for?" Killigan's
voice was hard and gravelly at the same time. It
was as though he was speaking not only with his
voice but with his shoulders and arms as well.

Cecil Dunbellamy thought he looked like a slab
of rock standing there, and just as impassive.

With an effort Cecil wiped the girl from his
mind, and wondered if his visitor could smell her
perfume lingering in the air as he could.

"I want you to take care of someone," he said.

Bowdrie Killigan didn't blink. "Is it the same sonofabitch I be thinkin' of?"

"I'd hazard that guess."

"You'd what?"

"I guess that's so."

"You got to pay me good for that one."

"We agreed on a price the last time we spoke, as I am sure you will remember."

"That was then. Things is different now. I want half again what you said."

"That's too much."

"Then get somebody else."

"Make it a quarter."

"No." And the big man turned on his heel.

"All right. All right then."

Killigan had stopped at the door, and now turned back to face Cecil Dunbellamy again.

"I'll do it my way then," Killigan said.

"No. I will tell you how."

Killigan shook his head and started to turn again, when Cecil held up his hand.

"Now just wait a minute. We will work this out. You don't know how I want the job done, so you shouldn't be so foolish as to refuse before you know what I want."

"Huh," said Killigan. And then again, "Huh."

"You listen carefully now. I will tell you exactly what I want and then we can discuss it. Though it's going to have to wait until tomorrow. I have another appointment right now."

"Tomorrow."

"Around noontime. I'll tell you my plan, and you can tell me yours. And we'll work it out.

What the devil, we both want to achieve the same end."

"Whaddaya mean?" asked Bowdrie Killigan.

"You'll see that what I desire isn't that much different—if at all—from what you wish."

"Shit, mister, I don't follow all that fancy high-falutin talk. You got to tell it to me straight."

"I will say it once again. What I want is exactly . . . . well, pretty much exactly what you want."

"Huh?" Killigan's brows, raised in question, formed deep furrows in his forehead. And Cecil suddenly realized that the man's seeming impassivity only masked a good deal of stupidity.

"I want you to humiliate him," Cecil Dunbellamy said. "I want you to bring him down. Do you understand me?"

And he caught the glint in the big man's eyes as he nodded. Then, without another word, Bowdrie Killigan turned, walked to the door, and opened it.

Cecil Dunbellamy closed it behind him, then locked it. He was smiling broadly, and his trousers were taut as he hurried to the other door that led to the room where his visitor was waiting.

"My dear, my apologies for taking so long."

"I'll only forgive you if you'll stop standing there and get into bed."

Cecil Dunbellamy had already started to pull off his clothes. His eyes were riveted on her as she lay in the bed, leaning on one arm, with her hand against her head. Her delicious breasts were not quite exposed to his eager eyes.

"I didn't think I could stand waiting so long," she gasped as he finally pulled off his trousers and stepped swiftly to the bed with his erection leading the way.

In a trice she had it in her mouth, sucking a long, slow, delicious stroke, and his legs gave away and he almost fell on top of her.

"Oh my God, my God," he gasped as she took it all the way into her throat. At the same time she reached one hand around to squeeze his buttock, while with the other she fondled his loaded balls.

He turned and buried his face in her dark bush, his tongue licking deep into her soaking lips. Her buttocks pumped in ecstasy, and in exact time with her own sucking.

She was moaning, unable to speak with his long, thick cock in her mouth, almost choking her. He himself could hardly breathe—and didn't care whether he did or not—with his face buried in her delicious bush.

Until finally and together they came, trying to hold it to the last, final, split second, enjoying the ultimate quiver and squirt of their delicious passion.

They collapsed, lying in their positions, she with his softening cock in her mouth, he with his face sunk into her soaking cunt. They slept. It had been a long day, and it had been almost all of twenty-four hours since they'd last spent their passion.

In a little while they stirred.

"Did you sleep?" she asked, addressing his limp penis.

He chuckled, knowing to whom she was speaking. "We both did," he said. "And you?"

"Ah, yes."

They turned now so that they faced each other and he put his arm around her.

"Are you tired?" he asked.

"I am."

Her eyes were shut and she was smiling up at the ceiling. He raised himself up on an elbow to look down at her. God, she was beautiful. Dark, skin like cream, large green eyes, closed now, but they were twin magnets. He pushed the sheet back and surveyed her big nipples, still red from his play, and her breasts big but springy, just right for his hand. He loved it when she bounced them in his face when they played their game; he would try to catch one in his mouth, while she wiggled away, defying and tantalizing him until it seemed he would go out of his mind and could stand not one second more of the exquisite torture.

He lay back and closed his eyes, and in the next moment he felt her hand on his stomach, moving down slowly, taking her time. And God how well she knew what to do!

He was stirring below and, as her fingers found his cock, then his balls, he was again erect. He, for his part, had reached over to caress her fur. She parted her legs and he felt her wetness, and his middle finger slipped easily into her soaking cunt.

And she was moaning, wiggling with mounting desire, as she pumped him with her fist, her hand sliding easily in the wet come and the smell of it invaded them both, driving them to further passion.

Turning closer to her their lips met and his tongue sank deep into her mouth, playing with her tongue, while their hands felt, and stroked, and squeezed, and each thought of nothing but what was happening right there and then.

"I want it doggie-way," she said, turning over and pulling up onto her hands and knees.

"Anyway you want it, my dear." And he was on his knees, guiding his bone-hard member right into her soaking slit. High and deep.

He stroked her slowly, bringing his cock right out, to just under its head,

"No . . . no. Don't take him out!" she cried, gasping and reaching back to grab his balls.

"Only playing, my dear. I wouldn't dream of disengaging myself from this delight. Do you think I'm crazy?"

"Oh my, oh my God, it's so good . . . good . . . good . . . !"

And he was thrusting and wiggling and she was keeping with him at each stroke, not losing him for a second—until again they came, and came, and came. . . .

They lay on their backs, tired, swept with satisfaction and unutterable joy.

"Christ, you're terrific," he said.

"Glad you think so, mister." And she snuggled her head into his shoulder.

This way they slept.

It seemed a good while later that he awakened. It seemed especially dark in the room. He had no idea how long they had slept. She was snuggled close to him, with her arm across his chest.

When he dropped his hand onto her hip she murmured.

"Couldn't hear you, my dear."

"I said I want it again."

"Again?"

"Mmmm."

And he was already playing with her bush, her wet lips, and stroking the inside of her thighs. Her hips began to undulate, and she reached over and held the head of his cock with her fingertips, tickling it right under its purple head.

"You're going to get it," he promised.

"How do you want it?" he said, his words coming out in spurts, it seemed, for he could hardly keep still, and he felt again that he was going to explode.

And again he marveled at her, not only at her capacity for passion—she seemed insatiable— but her ability to increase his own, for he never seemed to get enough. She was extraordinary.

"I want it doggie again," she said, gasping into his ear.

And he turned toward her and was on his hands and knees.

As was she, with her head down between her arms, and her buttocks high in the air, and her legs spread.

He entered her easily, sliding in all the way

to the hilt, touching bottom too, and rubbing the head of his still enormous erection until she moaned and all but cried out loud in her passion. He rode her gently, moving high up, then stroking low, then sideways back and forth, drawing his iron-hard member out to its head till she begged him not to leave. And then he began thrusting in and out, and in and out and faster and harder and high and deep and then faster and faster and faster . . . until they both squirted everything they had and sank down to rest on the tussled sheets, damp with their passion and smelling of come.

For the moment, Cecil Dunbellamy thought it was sufficient.

SEVEN

Clint Adams had awakened early, light just starting to appear on the windowsill of his hotel room. Still, even though he was invariably an early riser, he had a feeling of something already afoot.

He sat up, swung his legs over the side of the bed and stood. Fifteen minutes later he was seated in the Bucket Cafe waiting for his steak and potatoes and baking powder biscuits. He was already halfway through his first cup of coffee when he saw Ed Steiner walk in. And he knew that his early morning instinct had been right. There was no doubt that something must have caused such a feeling of apprehension in the town. Thus far, he had heard nobody say anything about anything special—— not the old man in the Bucket Cafe who'd been grousing back there in the kitchen, and not the clerk back at the hotel, nor any of the half dozen early morning people he'd seen in the street. Still, there was something going on. And here it was, he said to himself as the sheriff of Landers and the surrounding country walked swiftly to his table in a corner of the room.

"You heard the news, Adams?"

"Let me guess. A holdup?"

The sheriff grunted at this touch of humor in regard to the problem he was facing. The problem was not so much the bandits and the recovery of their loot, as much as the demand from Cecil Dunbellamy that he include the services of the man known as the Gunsmith.

"Adams, I got to tell you, I need all the help I can get. And that's a gut!" He sniffed, hawked, and spat powerfully into a nearby cuspidor. The Gunsmith admired his accuracy, especially knowing the lawman was under so much stress. "You mind what I am sayin'. I need every man, 'specially a man of substance. Which I know from your reputation you happen to be."

Clint immediately realized what was coming and decided that while in no way did he wish to be working with the law in the capacity of some kind of twenty-four-hour deputy, on the other hand such an adventure could very well open up some of the silence which had been greeting him in relation to Wayne Behrens, the railroads, and land-grabbers who were flooding the West with immigrants and promises.

"I might give you a hand," he said.

And Steiner's eyebrows lifted in surprise and, in a way, gratitude. He needed help, and he needed it badly. And with the Gunsmith siding with him he told himself that he felt a "whole helluva lot better," being one of those older men who indulged in self-discussion on just about everything and anything that crossed his path.

It wasn't long after dawn that the sheriff accompanied by Clint Adams and five other men and horses had formed a posse. A special engine and a freight car had been commandeered to carry them out to Bone Canyon, a distance of some thirty miles. The rain had stopped. The armed party led their horses down the ramp from the freight car and mounted.

"Thing to do," said Sheriff Steiner, "is figger which way the buggers went, and how far they gone."

Nobody present argued this unassailable point.

"They'd likely head north for the Montana country," someone suggested. "Wouldn't you reckon? I figure on the other side of Gebo Creek."

"What do you think, Adams?" The sheriff cocked an eye at Clint, who was paying close attention.

"I'd say they'll be pretty cocksure they won't be followed. They'd expect us to figure Gebo Creek and north, being as it's heading right into the high mountain country. See, they know they left no trail, on account of the rain. They know they weren't recognized. I'd suspect they planned on gettin' to some town—might even be there already."

"Which way you figger?" asked one of the men, pushing the brim of his Stetson hat up so he could take a closer look at the man who was a stranger to them, but who they'd all heard about from time to time.

"Well, they'd have to move West likely, least-ways at first. In this narrow canyon where they pulled the holdup it's the only likely way, when you consider the rain and darkness. The other way is blocked by those big boulders. We won't need a trail to follow them for a few miles any-way."

"That makes sense," Steiner allowed.

"Are there any outfits around here?" Clint asked.

"Sure are. Four, five," said Steiner. "What're you thinking?"

"They'll have to change horses. Can only ride so far and they'll figure that out quick."

"We could try Hiker's first," someone said.

"He's about the same distance as Dunnell," Steiner said. "He'd be more likely, if we figure the boys are from this part of the country, which I do believe we got to. They knew too much for anybody from out of the country to pull the job."

"You know this Dunnell, do you?" Clint asked.

"He's none too bright. They'd figure they could bulldoze Dunnell easier'n anybody else."

Dunnell, it turned out, was a humble rancher-farmer, and Steiner said he was well liked around Landers. The posse found him at home, relaxing on his front porch, smoking his pipe. Ed Steiner rode forward, while Clint Adams hung back, lis-tening to the exchange.

"How come you ain't out working your stock?" the sheriff asked.

"Don't feel too good this day. Somethin' I et, I figger."

"You had any callers?"

"No. Nary a one. Whyn't you boys step down and set a spell. Got coffee inside on the stove. Maybe some biscuits. I'm batchin' since the missus went to visit folks over in Sills."

"We'll just rest our hosses a spell, while we visit with you. Coffee sounds good, eh, boys?" And, turning in his saddle, the sheriff noted that Clint Adams had drawn away and was walking his horse toward the small creek that ran about a hundred yards on the north side of the house.

Clint had exchanged a look with Steiner just before he peeled away from the group and now the sheriff kept their host well engaged in conversation. He dismounted and led Duke to a trough into which water could be ladled from a spring. He stood quietly, watching the horse as he drank. He did not appear to be looking for anything special, and was very careful not to arouse suspicion on the part of their host.

Clint had noticed of course that the corral was empty, and took note of it, wondering where Dunnell's horse might be. Well, maybe in the barn. One side of the corral was a rock cliff some twenty feet high, but the cliff extended on past the fence for two or three miles, right into open grazing land. He started to walk out along the bluff, marking again how the corral had been empty.

He was not much more than a quarter mile out when he came upon a horse. It was a bay, with a white forehead and three white stockings. It was huddled against the cliff, head down. Clint edged in closer. It was clear to him that the horse was sick or in the last stages of exhaustion. He also noted that sweat had dried on it. The cliff had obviously kept it out of the last rain showers which would otherwise have washed off any sweat.

Next, he climbed the cliff. About half a mile away he spotted two more horses, just standing where they were, not moving at all; it was as though they were exhausted. He turned then and walked back to the house.

When he walked in, Ed Steiner looked up from his stool and said, "You look like a man who's found somethin' interestin'." And he cocked an eye at their host who suddenly looked uncomfortable.

"I found some half-dead horses out there," the Gunsmith said, looking at Dunnell. And his tone was grim. "One was still sweating, and the other two I saw didn't have your brand on them."

At this point, Ed Steiner straightened in his seat, clearly to have a free draw with his handgun if necessary.

"Better start talkin', Dunnell," he said, and his voice was not friendly.

Dunnell glanced nervously at Clint Adams.

"Better talk," Clint said. "There was killing. And it wasn't hosses."

Dunnell's forehead was glistening.

"Told you they'd kill you, did they? Somethin'
like that?" Ed Steiner said.

Dunnell nodded. He knew the men. And they
had sworn that if he talked to anybody they would
come back and slit his throat.

"It was Harold Tripe, one of the Blackjack gang,"
he said, and his voice faltered with his fear. "He—
he smacked me some. Hell, Ed, you know I ain't
no spring chicken anymore. An' I got family too.
Amy an' the two are in town."

"So they took your horses," Clint said, cutting
in, wanting to get to the point fast. He did not at
all approve of men who treated their horses the
way these had been treated.

"Yes, yes, they took them."

"Where they headed?" asked Steiner.

"For the Hell Hole."

"They told you? I don't believe it." Steiner
snorted.

"They didn't say it to me," Dunnell said and his
face, which had been red, now paled consider-
ably. "I heard them talking to themselves. They
was arguing it. They'd been drinking. Fact, they
was real drunk."

Clint looked at Steiner. "You know him, Sheriff."

Steiner nodded, and now his look was hard as
a gun barrel as he addressed Dunnell. "You know
you better not be lyin' about this. I mean, you
better know you should be more scared of me
and this gentleman here than you are of those
mangy cutthroats you gave hosses to. You goddam fool!"

"I didn't give them!" Dunnell half rose from his chair in protest. "I didn't give. They took. The sonofbitches took 'em! They by God didn't give a royal shit. They just took!" He was almost in tears, and Clint realized he must have packed away a snootful himself right after the boys rode out.

Ed Steiner knew the place called the Hell Hole.

"It's actually no more'n a hole among some rocks," he snorted. None of the posse men had ever heard of the Hell Hole, so Steiner explained that it was a cave around which ignorant people like Dunnell had built superstitions. An old trapper from the old, old days was supposed to live down in the hole, Steiner explained to Clint. An old man who had come there three hundred years ago and had found a stream of eternal life under ground.

"The ghosts we'll find, if any, won't be three hundred years old," the sheriff said. "Come to think of it, that's a pretty good place if they mean to hide out."

"But it ain't no place for a body to live any length of time," one man in the posse argued. "I wouldn't be surprised if they were just lying to throw Dunnell off."

"Then how about those tracks in that mud?" asked the sheriff, pointing. "They've only been sprinkled on."

And Clint nodded, seeing that sure enough, tracks of four horses showed plainly in the soil. Tracks obviously made just before the rain had stopped in the early morning.

Some while later, they approached the Hell Hole, which Ed Steiner explained to the group had originally been called the Ghost Hole—for some reason he'd almost forgotten that fact. Then the posse deployed, rifles in hand. "No need to take chances," Steiner warned.

Ed Steiner led the way, Clint Adams bringing up the rear. And it was the Gunsmith who spotted the horses. They were hobbled and grazing down the slope.

"Those be Dunnell's horses, by damn!" said Steiner.

"And the boys will likely be expecting us," Clint Adams said, cautioning the group to draw rein. "Unless they're fast asleep—all of them—they'll have spotted us. That's a place not likely to be found unbeknownst."

"Maybe I can slip up on that side yonder," said the sheriff.

At that instant a rifle shot cracked from the mouth of the cave.

The sheriff's horse reared, screamed once, and fell. Steiner narrowly escaped getting a broken leg. He drew his six-gun swiftly and, cursing, shot the animal to end its suffering.

The men in the cave answered with further rifle fire. And now the men of the posse answered with a fierce round of their own. They dismounted to seek cover, then literally poured bullets back at the black entrance to the Hell Hole.

To be sure the bandits were safe behind the high rocks. And they were obviously well armed, firing back rapidly. One posse man was struck in the shoulder as he crawled up the hill, seeking a better spot for firing at the bandits.

The remaining six lay prone, taking no chances. For half an hour or so the exchange of bullets kept up with no evident casualty on either side.

Finally, the Gunsmith crawled over to Steiner. "I'd like to try something, Sheriff."

"Shit, man. That's what I been waitin' for."

Clint ignored the caustic remark. But his answer was not exactly sweet. "Then get someone to go get some dynamite."

"Not a bad idea," the sheriff said. "But I dunno where you could get a stick of dynamite within a hundred miles of this place."

Clint didn't answer him. Instead he cupped his hands to his mouth and shouted, off to his side, slightly away from the Hell Hole. "Billy, you and Fred go back and get that dynamite I left at Dunnell's. Move yer asses now!"

"You believe they're gonna swallow that one, do ya?" asked Steiner, incredulously.

"Why not?"

"Best thing would be to starve 'em out, but that'll take a while, and—shit—I got to get back to town."

"Go ahead. And bring some dynamite back with you, or send it," Clint said sourly.

"You want to stay here?"

"I am not heading up this posse," the Gunsmith said. "That's your job, and if you want to go back and call the whole thing off, that's all right with me. I just came along for the ride anyway."

They squatted now by a small fire that one of the men had built, and cooked up some Arbuckle's coffee, and ate beef jerky.

It was close to twilight when Clint Adams approached the posse men seated around the tiny camp fire.

"What you got in the sack there?" somebody asked. "I'd like a couple of steaks myself."

A rough chuckle ran around the group, for the men were clearly tired and hungry. Clint had sent one of the men back to Dunnell's for food, and to send a message to Landers that they were pinning down the bandits.

"I got to get back in the forenoon," Ed Steiner was saying to Clint for the third or fourth time. It was clear to the Gunsmith that the man was under strong pressure.

The sheriff was looking at the sack that Clint was holding, having just taken it from the rider who'd gone back to Dunnell's. "What *is* in that thing?" he asked.

"Since you want to know, it's dynamite I picked up at the train job and left at Dunnell's outfit. Those knotheads who pulled that job were dumb to leave their extra dynamite around. I brought it along, figuring we might find a use for it. For instance, right now."

He watched the surprise in Ed Steiner's face as he said those words—it was clearly there. He could see the whole layout now.

He had just lifted his head a little higher to take in the lowering sun on the distant mountain top when something—his extra sense, he called it—

warned him and he spun, catching the glint from a gun barrel. Dropping to his knee and drawing, he got off three shots, while the rifleman's bullet with Clint Adams' name on it went whining into the sapphire sky.

But the man who fired the shot did not. He stood up—unaccountably, it seemed to Clint—and then tumbled forward, his rifle falling onto the rocks that had hidden him. His gun clattered once, and then slid down the hard-packed trail just below his hiding place.

"You'll find him dead," the Gunsmith said as he reloaded his six-gun and slipped it back into its holster.

He walked to his horse and checked his saddle rigging. Then he stepped into the stirrup, swung up and over, and settled easily into the saddle.

He looked down at the surprise on Sheriff Ed Steiner's face. "Be careful you don't lose any of that express car loot on your way back to Landers, Sheriff."

"Where you going? And what about the dynamite?"

"They likely have got it all with them in their cave," Clint said.

The sheriff looked just slightly puzzled. "How did you figure it out, mister?"

Clint Adams leaned forward on the pommel of his stock saddle, crossing his forearms. "Easy enough. Number one, you just seemed a bit too sure on where to find the boys. Number two, old man Dunnell was easy enough to see through. That's not his outfit, in the first place. He couldn't find his way around that kitchen if he had a map. And he spoke of his wife, like she'd just been there. He doesn't have a wife. I can tell when a man's been batching no more'n five, ten minutes after I been in his cabin." He sniffed. "Tell your buddy Dunbellamy, he'll have to do better than that." He sat back in his saddle and lifted his reins.

He was about to knee Duke into a walk, but he didn't. Instead he leaned forward again and looked directly down at Ed Steiner.

"Your fake train holdup might fool a lot of people. But if you ever intend to try that on me again, you damn well better do a decent job." Reaching to his shirt pocket he took out the makings and began building himself a smoke.

Ed Steiner watched him, not able to hide the amazement in his face.

"You're wrong, Adams. That was a real holdup. There's two dead men back there to prove it."

"Oh, the job was real. I don't doubt that. But I do believe you'll find the men you're supposed to be looking for . . . well . . ." he squinted at the sky. "I'd say they was probably bellyin' up for drinks in one or another of those fine drinking places in Landers right about now. If they haven't been celebrating already." He grinned. "Give Mr. Dunbellamy some advice from me. Tell him next time he wants to fool somebody with one head 'stead of two and a half heads, he'll have to do a whole lot better than using those three knotheads who tried gulching me a few days back down by Morgan's Crossing. That one with the rifle, had the same whine from a loose firing pin—just like this one today."

And he sat there watching the surprise cover the whole of Ed Steiner's face.

"Jesus God," said the sheriff of Landers. "You for sure know your guns, doncha, mister." And his jaw was hanging open in surprise.

Clint Adams settled back in his saddle, lifting his reins and kneeing Duke. "Reckon that's why they call me the Gunsmith, Sheriff."

There was no question but that Landers, Wyoming Territory was going to celebrate the glorious Fourth of July in the traditional high-spirited way. It was that very afternoon that Clint Adams stepped out of Sheriff Ed Steiner's office and started down the street toward his hotel. He had just told Steiner that he wanted no further part of any "deputy games," and that if he, Steiner, ran across Cecil Dunbellamy he could damn well tell him so.

Actually, the Gunsmith was more than pleased with the way things had turned out in their pursuit of the gang that had held up the Northern Pacific. The action at the Hell Hole had given him a good view of Sheriff Ed Steiner, and the kind of men he was able to call as deputies, and also he'd caught a good angle on how Mr. Cecil Dunbellamy operated. More confirmation than fresh news, the Northern Pacific man showed he didn't hesitate to deal from the bottom, middle, or even the honest top of the deck if it suited his purpose. Clint Adams also realized fully that the man was utterly ruthless but, like just about everyone else, he had a weak spot. It was the usual weak spot of the big dealers. Now he was glad to have the Fourth as an opportunity to get a picture of the entire town, more or less as a whole.

Nearly all the residents of not only Landers, but also nearby Homer, were there to stare and wonder at the balloon ascension, the freaks and fire-eaters, and to marvel at the fantastic performance of The Great Gramboni.

A large crowd had gathered to watch The Great One as he gracefully pedaled along the tightrope, back and forth, high above the heads of the astonished onlookers. The Great Gramboni, veteran that he was, seemed not in the least fazed at being the center of attention. Totally at ease, his flowing black handlebar mustache never quivered, while his enormous bald head shone like an astounding beacon under the afternoon sunlight.

Clint Adams had been watching from the edge of the crowd. He had a rather exceptional view of all the action, especially the drama that was being enacted on the other side of the street. When he stepped up onto the boardwalk for a better look, he saw two men bearing down swiftly on a man who was about to mount a big dappled gray horse. All at once the man withdrew his foot from the stirrup, drew his six-shooter and fired. But the other two men were quicker, and more accurate. The gunman, caught in the act of making off with horseflesh that was not his, was shot dead with his boots on.

A great shout arose from the crowd. This was not because of the sudden death of a horse thief, but rather because The Great Gramboni, himself distracted by the foiled horse theft beneath him, had suddenly lost his balance and had gone plunging to the ground. But he had the good fortune to be intercepted, landing in a wagon box filled with sacks of flour. When he rose, he found his breath knocked out of him to the extent that he was unable to swear at his predicament and could only emit small, coughing grunts. Dusted white with flour, he had reaped a narrow escape. As he came to his knees in the wagon box a great cheer broke from the crowd. In addition, the law earned a round of applause itself for bringing a prospective horse thief to ultimate justice.

Eager hands helped The Great Gramboni descend from the flour wagon, and he was again roundly cheered. However, almost instantly his bright smile turned to gloom as a group of furious gamblers descended on him. They had bet heavily on his success. Fortunately, for the moment, their displeasure remained verbal and others, thrilled by the closeness of tragedy in the form of death or at least mangling, swept the high-wire artiste, as he was billed, to the nearest saloon.

Figuring that the excitement of the Fourth of July plus the imbibing of strong spirits would surely loosen a number of tongues, Clint Adams followed the crowd to O'Toole's. Here, he found The Great Gramboni, still dusted with a generous amount of flour, arguing hotly with his promoter who, because of his fall was trying to get out of paying him.

In a little while the crowd around him began to drift back into the street and when the Gunsmith approached, The Great One was calming his annoyance and hurt vanity with strong booze.

He was a solid man, The Gramboni was: broadshouldered, yet nimble almost as a professional dancer. He informed Clint Adams that he had been born in an Italian circus touring Russia at the time. His mother was Greek, his father Italian. He had traveled all over the world—Turkey, London, Paris—with various troupes, performing before crowned heads. He was, he said quite simply, the world's greatest highwire artiste. But he was concerned—no, worried—about his pay and about the gamblers who had lost money on him.

"Might be a good notion to get yourself out of town for a spell," Clint suggested. "There's a good bit of drinking about and I have seen crowds get real nasty with the booze in them, especially when there's money involved."

The Great One touched the two ends of his waxed mustache with his thumb and middle finger. He shrugged, raising his thick eyebrows.

"You think there could be trouble?" he asked suddenly, forgetting his Italian-Russian accent in the moment of stress.

"I am saying it might be a good notion to lie low for a spell."

"Ah, but where? I have no money. They have not paid me." He drummed his fingers on the top of the bar. "In fact, my friend, I must ask you to purchase me another drink."

The Gunsmith liked that. The man put on a pretty fake act, but he had the feeling that he was pretty straight inside.

At just that moment they heard a shout going up in the street, followed by the thudding of horses' hooves and then gunfire.

"God Almighty!" said The Great Gramboni. "This place, it is indeed the Wild West like everybody says it is!"

But Clint Adams had already walked quickly to the door to catch the shouting of the crowd as the midday stage from Calhoun Junction came in.

He heard the cries of "Holdup!" and "Bandits!" and then lots of yelling as the stage pulled up outside Ed Steiner's office in a sheet of heavy dust.

And there was Steiner himself swearing, red-faced and sweating, dressing down the driver for running his team and stage down the main street of town.

"Jesus H. Christ, Paltry! What the hell you think you doin' You know better'n to run yer hosses in a dry street. You tryin to cover this whole town in dust, fer Chrissakes!"

Little Phil Paltry was standing up, almost before he had pulled his horses to a stop. His face was red and wet with perspiration and excitement.

For the moment Clint was glad to get out of the saloon. It had been hot, and it was always exciting to meet the stage. And he even felt a touch of regret that the railroads would soon supplant the old stagelines. However, he was a practical man too, and realized the many benefits of traveling in

the Iron Horse—as the Indians were calling it—
compared to the rigors of stagecoach travel.

The stage had hardly pulled up behind the
sweating team of horses when Little Phil and
the big man riding shotgun, Big Joe Miller, had
jumped down to help the passengers who had
clearly been through a very rough time at the
hands of the road agents.

A large crowd had gathered, larger than usual
because it was coupled with the Fourth of July
festivities.

The passengers were obviously shaken, especially the middle-aged couple who first descended.
The man was helping his wife, who held a handkerchief to her mouth.

They were followed by another man, who was
also trying to help the woman. Clint had pretty
well summed up what had happened. It was
more or less the classic holdup, judging from
the conversation that was going on in a loud
voice between the driver, the shotgun guard, and
Sheriff Ed Steiner. A sudden shot had been fired
across the front of the horses and the demand
made to pull up. Then two masked men appeared
but there were obviously others who were out of
sight, covering. A hat was passed for the passengers to throw in their valuables, and the warning
was given not to attempt pursuit—as if that were
possible. Then the men swiftly departed taking
the guards' weapons and the six-gun carried by
the driver, along with a handgun from one of the
passengers. There was another male passenger,
who also answered questions from the onlookers

and Steiner as he descended from the coach.

The Gunsmith was about to turn away when one more passenger appeared. And the crowd suddenly quieted in surprise. It was the sight of the final passenger that brought a silence to the crowd of onlookers as only a special beauty can.

Clint Adams felt something turn over inside him when he saw her, something that he hadn't felt in—as he put it to himself—some good while.

She looked at nobody, though he could tell she had taken in the crowd and the town at a glance. She paused a moment to speak to the handler from the stage office who was taking down the baggage. And Clint Adams found himself hoping that she would be staying at his hotel, but, he reasoned, she must be staying with friends; for nobody that good looking would be coming to such a place as Landers to be alone.

He watched as she instructed the boy about her baggage and the boy, in turn, pointed in the direction of The Wranglers Rest. Clint Adams was on the verge of walking over to ask if he might carry her luggage, but the boy was already engaged in handling it.

He caught again the way she moved, the graceful line of her arm as she pointed at her bags, and the way she carried her head. Yet, try as he might, he was not able to catch a full view of her face. Yet he knew it. He could imagine it. And he felt his breath catch again while his eyes followed her down the street as she walked just a step behind the boy who was carrying her two pieces of luggage.

He remained where he was, while the small knot of people now melted back into the larger crowd of July Fourth celebrants.

Suddenly, Ed Steiner was beside him.

"Like a word with you, if you've a mind to," the sheriff said easily.

Clint turned slowly to look at the lawman. "Why?"

"Some things ain't settled. Got a bit too hairy out there at the Hell Hole. Didn't mean to . . . well, push you away. Mr. Dunbellamy wants to see you."

"He's seen me, and I've seen him," Clint said. "And I reckon we've seen each other enough."

"What am I gonna tell him?"

"Tell him what I just told you."

"He ain't gonna like it."

"You're breaking my heart." He started to walk away, but stopped and turned around to face the sheriff of Landers again.

"You can tell him something if you've a mind to," he said.

Ed Steiner nodded. "Good enough," he said.

"Tell him to go piss up a rope."

EIGHT

The Wyoming Wranglers Rest, to give the hotel its full name, had been moved to Landers from Barnaby Junction just one year before the railroad spur of the Northern Pacific led the generous building boom, not to mention the growing population of immigrants from Europe. Families of men, women, children, grandparents, cousins, not to forget singles, had caught the fever of the West, had read the advertisements crying the advantages, the excitement, the riches of the Great American West. There was free land for farming, raising cattle, wheat, barley. The topsoil was inches thick, the land bursting with wealth to be dug, farmed, grown, coaxed, prayed over—yes, just for the asking. The land was begging for humans to take it and reap the great riches that were simply oozing from the richest topsoil ever. From all over Europe the people came, escaping the worn-out, farmed-out, absolutely exploited land of Europe, and Russia. They came from all the corners of the Old World, which was now shriveled from overuse, greed, weariness, and the pressure of more mouths than it could possibly feed.

They came to the land of plenty, clutching their life savings and the literature that told them of heaven on earth that was there simply for the asking, the land of opportunity. Helped by the beneficence of the great American railroads, the great land promoters, and the great emotions engendered by the word *freedom*, they came West.

"If you didn't see it for yourself, you wouldn't believe it," Fifield Wister said to the Gunsmith as they sat in the office of *The Landers Bugle*, of which Fifield was publisher, editor, and, in fact, chief scrivener; that is to say, he was boss and staff all in one. This setup was the consequence of not only a wise economy for Fifield, but also an assurance that whatever was written for the *Bugle* would be intelligent, entertaining, and assuredly humorous; the Fifield sense of humor was famous, and not infrequently feared throughout the Territory.

"It'd be pretty damn hard not to see it," Clint Adams said, as he settled in his chair and accepted the generous drink that his host passed to him along with the bottle, from which both had been imbibing for some time.

Clint was enjoying himself. He'd spotted Fifield Wister early on as a man to get to know. He obviously had a keen sense of humor, and from what Clint had read in the *Bugle*, he could see the man was literate, intelligent, humorous, and—

he would have bet—reasonably honest. At the
same time, the publisher and editor and chief
writer of the *Bugle* was no rebellious do-gooder
who planned to educate and change the ways of
mankind. It was obvious to the Gunsmith that
Wister had the sensitivity to see things as they
were and the level head to leave life and people as they were, accepting them within reason,
and reporting on same with humor, wisdom, and
taste.

"They've been scouring Europe with their
broadsides, as you surely know, Adams," Wister
was saying, "and one is caught momentarily with
a sense of outrage at the charlatans. Right now the
rubes are beginning to see—of course too late—
that they've been rooked, chiseled, and screwed
out of their life savings, sold a bill of goods saying that the topsoil was so deep and theirs for
the asking . . ." And he held his hands far apart
to indicate the alleged depth of the topsoil in
hard-rock Wyoming and other western territories.
"Only to discover too late that it was all bullshit
and they've lost their life savings. The famous
topsoil was barely an inch deep and has already
blown off to leave . . ." He opened his hands in an
offering gesture. "Hardpan. A bare inch of topsoil,
which the winds blew and blew and blew away.
They will see this again and again. The railroads,
my friend, and the politicians, are screwing the
country." He paused, and reached for his drink.
"I have been informed that you recently rode out
and took a look at some of the railwork going on
over at Gunner's Pass." He paused, pursing his

lips, his brow raised into ridges, like a corrugated roadbed, Clint Adams thought, his mind on the shoddy railroad work he had seen.

"It'll not hold up, if you ask me," he said.

His host nodded. "Of course, you know who's paying for this caper."

"The taxpayers."

Fifield Wister nodded, pursed his lips, and opened the cigar box that was on his desk within easy reach even though he was not sitting in his usual place, but in a visitor's chair like his companion. "The government is under pressure and receiving paybacks from the railroads. And both of them are trying to gobble up what is left. In point of fact, all the railroads throughout the entire country—but especially the Northern Pacific—are making millions in real estate. From land that is supposed to belong to the public.

"I see that. And as for the work being done at Gunner's Pass, well it's of course done in the name of being first to connect with the Western when they join."

"The Union Transcontinental is doing the same thing," Wister said. "They want to beat the N.P. The whole damn railroad will have to be rebuilt probably even sooner than we think."

"And the law?" Clint said. "The law knows this?"

"You are joking perhaps," said his host with a smile. "The law *is* this. Steiner, Fort Larrabee, Washington, Cheyenne, the whole kit and caboodle are in on this boondoggle, my friend. And your man knew about it."

"My man?"

"Your man Jake Shore."

Clint was nodding slowly. "I'd begun to figure something like that." He looked closely at
Wister now, leaning forward with his elbows on
his knees. "Did you know Wayne Behrens?"

"I did. He was a good man. Or is. I dunno
which. Heard he was shot up." And he looked
questioningly at the Gunsmith.

"He got it," Clint said, looking down at his
hands. "There was a chance he was going to
make it. But that's what I've come up here about.
He'd asked me to, but he cashed in before he had
a chance to go into detail."

"Hmm . . . and I can guess you haven't exactly
been received with wide open arms," said Fifield
Wister sourly. "Well, there's not much I can tell
you." He held up his hand suddenly to stop any
swift reply from his guest. "I mean by that, I can
tell you plenty, but I can't prove it. And listen,
Adams . . ." He leaned forward with his forearms
on his knees. "I have told you nothing. Nothing!
It's all speculation. I can't prove a thing. And
even if I could go to Washington and Cheyenne
and tell them . . . hell, man, everybody knows it
already. Yes, as yourself knew it. It's right in front
of everyone's eyes how the N.P. is stealing the
land, diddling the public and getting away with
millions! But of course, it isn't only the railroads,
it's the land companies. The bullshit about building the 'Great American West' . . . let me tell you,
Adams, let me tell you . . ." He paused to refill his
glass and his visitor's. "Let me tell you . . . you say
anything to anybody about what I've told you and

I will deny it all the way! I promise you that!" He was suddenly furious, and Clint could see how the drink had gotten to him.

"I have heard nothing from you," the Gunsmith said. "Nothing that I didn't know already. Hell, man, I am not deaf, dumb, or blind. Or stupid, let me add! Nor is anybody else. So leave it. Let's leave it. I have seen nothing I can prove. I am only here to round out a report that my friend—yes, my friend asked of me. When I'm done I'll turn my report—written with his knowledge, his backing, his blessing—to Fort Larrabee and be shut of it. And I'll then ride off into the great western sunset." He stood up.

"Got it?" He held out his hand, and his host rose, with a bit of alcoholic difficulty and accepted the shake.

"Sorry, Adams. I got a bit steamed there. Can't help it. I just hate seeing the bastards get away with it."

"Who says they're getting away with anything?" Clint asked.

"You know what would happen if I wrote up in the *Bugle* what I've just been telling you!"

"My friend, if you wrote it in the *Bugle*, screamed it from the housetops, it wouldn't cut any ice at all. Everybody knows it already. If they don't, it would come as little surprise to them. It's the way it is. Sure, the West, the frontier is being exploited. All over the place. But it's getting built. And it seems that's the only way it will get built. With guns, with fists. And then it will settle. You can't scramble a couple or three eggs without breaking the shells, my friend. I don't condone it, I don't agree with it. But it's a fact of life. Now then . . ." He leaned forward, reaching to his shirt pocket for his papers and tobacco sack. "Now then, how we gonna do it?"

Fifield Wister was staring at him goggle-eyed. "Do what?"

"How are we going to bust this wide open and show these sidewinders for what they are. See, you can't change the world, and you sure as hell can't change the people." He sat back, letting his words sink in.

"Well, by God, you sure as hell can't change people—or events," growled Fifield Wister, and his face had reddened. "So what're you going to do, Mr. Smart? Eh?" And he sat back and jammed his hands in his pockets and crossed one leg over the other. "So what can you do about it!" he repeated, and Clint caught the triumph in his voice. "Tell me," Fifield went on. "I want to know your secret, by God!"

"It's simple," the Gunsmith said, his voice calm, low, and his whole body relaxed as he sat easy in his chair.

"Tell!" said Wister impatiently, with a sneer in his voice this time. "Tell it then!"

"I can't change anybody, but I am sure as hell not gonna let 'em change me! That's number one."

"So what's number two?"

The Gunsmith was looking at his host as though he was simply gazing at the sky to remark on the weather. His voice was soft, and he was sitting absolutely still in his wooden chair. "Number two is simply understanding I can't do a damn thing about anything or about any another person."

"The hell . . . !"

"I can't do a thing," repeated Clint. "But what I can do is see what can be done."

"Jesus . . ."

"Mister . . . you can't stop a charging buffalo coming right at you. But you can sure as hell get out of his way!"

A silence suddenly filled the office now, as the Gunsmith finished speaking and sat back in his chair. He had finished building his smoke, and now struck a match one-handed on his thumbnail.

He held the lighted match for a moment without touching it to the cigarette which was hanging from the corner of his mouth. Then bending his head slightly, he touched the flame to the end of his smoke.

"We need a few more facts," the Gunsmith said as he exhaled his first drag. "You want to help this town from getting wiped out. Right?"

Fifield Wister nodded. "The land speculators are the ones I'm concerned with mostly."

"They're the ones we're talking about." Clint took a slow drag on his cigarette, then took it carefully out of his mouth and looked at the ash. "How does the town council, or whatever you call them, feel about all this?" he asked.

"They're all one hundred percent for it. Just so long as they can rake in the good old dollars they're happy. They don't see, they don't want to see what it's going to do to the country, the town,

the people. Those damn real estate buggers are
sewing us all into a body bag." He coughed suddenly, hawked, and spat into the cuspidor next to
his chair. "Tell me what's going to happen when
this town goes bust, when they see they're going
to have to rebuild not only the N.P. spur but more
than likely a sizeable chunk of the main line to
boot!"

"Who's behind it? It's Dunbellamy, isn't it."

"He's whipsawing it; that's for sure. But who's
behind him, I dunno. The bigwigs at Northern
Pacific maybe. But also some real estate interests.
And too, there's always the political bunch who
want power. Bigger the town, bigger the power."

"What about Fort Larrabee?" Clint asked suddenly.

The question startled his host. "Fort Larrabee?
But that's army."

"I know."

"I don't see what you're driving at."

"I'm not sure myself," Clint admitted. "But I do
know that these kinds of dice games often go for
the real big win. I am talking about that bright
yellow metal they call gold."

"Gold!"

"The yellow stuff."

"There's no gold around here. Shit, all you've
got here is the weather!"

"I'm not saying there is gold around here,"
Clint said. "But to attract people to a particular town . . . well, a gold rush would sure do it.
Wouldn't you say?" He looked closely at the newspaperman. "What would you say?"

"I'd say that is sure a way to do it. No question. Gold, silver, a strike of thousand dollar bills, sure, people'd come. But what are you getting at? I still say there's no gold in this part of the country." He was looking closely at his companion now. "But what have you heard? Why do you bring that up? About gold? "Have you seen it?"

Clint took the dead cigarette out of his mouth, and rolled the remaining tobacco and paper between his thumb and forefinger, then dropped the little ball into the cuspidor that was nearby.

"I've seen a shipment of picks and shovels. In Hogarth Petersen's store. I mean, a big shipment."

"Huh," said Fifield Wister, as he pondered this. "Huh."

"I don't reckon those picks are for anybody's teeth," the Gunsmith said. "And those shovels aren't the kind for shovelin' horseshit." He paused, grinning.

"Gold could be it," said Fifield Wister, looking down at his hands. "Jesus God. Can you imagine what it'll be like around here if there was a gold hit?"

"Excepting, maybe they are," Clint Adams mused.

Wister stared at him, puzzled. "What the hell are you talking about?" he asked. "Excepting maybe what are?" he asked, repeating the Gunsmith's sentence.

"For shoveling horseshit."

"What the hell you talking about!"

"I said that those kinds of shovels that I saw in Petersen's store aren't the kind for shoveling horseshit," he said, and he smiled a big smile at his host.

"What're you grinning about? The closest we ever came to a gold strike around Landers, or even any of the country around here was on Fool's Creek about a couple of years ago. But it was all over and done with in a couple of days. Just rumor."

"You don't get my point," Clint said. "I was saying that those shovels aren't the kind for shoveling horseshit."

"I heard you."

"But now I am saying that maybe they are."

"Are what?'" asked Fifield Wister, his tone of voice flecked with rising exasperation.

"Are for shoveling horseshit," said the Gunsmith. "Now stop being so thickheaded."

Maybe he was playing a hunch. Maybe it was just a move in order to keep moving. The Gunsmith, in any case, was never a man to waste his time, and he felt that there was a purpose in riding out to the cemetery.

He went early. The first sunlight was just topping the distant rimrocks when he reached the place allotted to the dead. It was, of course, on the outskirts of town. The graves were well away from the living, yet were in a quiet strip of land between two creeks, with juniper bushes along one side of the plot of special ground.

He had not known Jake Shore all that well. Yet he'd received a good impression of the man whenever he had run into him. Once at the big Z Bar T

up near Meeteetse and the Big Horn country, he'd
worked a couple of herds with Jake. And later
he'd discovered that Jake had started working
with Wayne Behrens. He'd known Wayne a long
time, and knew that he wouldn't be working with
a man unless said man measured up. It was clear
that Jake Shore had.

And he'd been shot. Dry-gulched, same as
Wayne, the sonsofbitches. The sonsofbitches, he
repeated to himself, changing slightly his empha-
sis on the word.

He found the plot with the wooden marker and
he wondered who had put it there. He had no
idea if Jake had any family, or even where he was
from. All he'd known about Jake Shore was that
he was a good man. And he was sorry he was
gone.

Suddenly he felt something change in the
atmosphere, and he stood very still, checking
again exactly where the sun was if he should turn.
He sure didn't want it in his eyes. But he was at
once alert to everything he needed, knowing that
everything he needed was right here. It had to be.

Now he heard a step. It wasn't heavy. Maybe a
woman? He turned, ready for anything. And he
almost gulped. It was the girl he had seen leaving
the stage.

She came slowly toward him, and she was still a
good distance away. He wondered if she had seen
him at the stage depot. She was wearing a simple
calico dress, but didn't move like somebody from
the country around Landers. He wasn't quite sure
how he meant that; yet he was sure of it. At the

same time she wasn't from one of the big cities either.

And then he realized that she was indeed heading toward him, evidently for Jake Shore's grave. Of course there were others, but this was the fresh one and she was a stranger in Landers. That much was obvious. And therefore. . . .

"Can you help me?" She was standing only a few feet from him now and he was fully aware of her good looks. She had dark hair and large brown eyes, that had a rather somber look, which was to be expected in a graveyard visit. Her body however, was soft and young. He guessed she was in her middle twenties. She was—well, delightful. But he quickly remembered his surroundings and quieted his excitement; at least he did his best to try to hide its external evidence.

"I will if I can," he said. "Help you." And she was so good-looking he didn't know whether to smile or not, considering the circumstances. And for an instant as she looked at him he felt a little foolish. But this swiftly passed as she smiled and said, "I'm looking for a new grave. . . . Someone named Shore." And then suddenly she caught herself, and almost blushed. "Oh, I'm sorry . . . I must have interrupted you, I am sorry . . ."

"It's right here," Clint said, nodding toward the simple wooden cross. "And you're not disturbing me at all." He quickly stepped back and away, for he realized his body had been in the way of her seeing the grave properly.

She looked, and something softened in her. It was very clear, her sorrow welling up in her. And she was holding a handkerchief in her hand.

Clint Adams could see this was no time to strike up an acquaintance with the girl, though he could not help admiring everything that was visible: the curve of her cheek, the way she bent her head, her soft hair, the way she was standing, her sorrow. . . .

Gently he withdrew.

He hoped that she would depart soon and he could meet her, for clearly she was a relative or friend of Jake. But he didn't wish to interfere, and so he retreated.

He was about halfway down the little trail back to the town when he heard the steps behind him and he stopped and turned. His first impression was again how lovely she looked. She was obviously sad, but her face was lovely and her figure was most attractive.

And so he waited until she came up to him. She nodded without smiling, for he could see that she'd been crying at least a little.

"I'm an old friend of Jake's," he said. "I hope I wasn't in the way there."

And then she smiled. "Of course not, and I for my part was concerned that possibly I'd scared you away." And then she suddenly blushed. "Oh, I didn't mean 'scared,' sir. I meant. . . . Well, I don't know what I meant except what I said."

And they were both laughing.

"I'm Jake's sister."

He peered at her. "I see."

"Half sister, so we don't really look much alike. Or didn't," she added.

They were walking down the path now, side by side, and Clint was feeling better than he had in days. So Jake had had a sister. Well, he'd never mentioned it. But then, why should he have said so?

"Will you be in Landers long?" he asked. "I was—"

"I don't know," she said. "Oh, excuse me! I interrupted you." She looked remorseful and, the Gunsmith thought, thoroughly delightful.

"No, you didn't interrupt me. It was I—"

"No, well, you see . . . oh, dear me, where was I?"

"You were back at the part where you'd thought you'd interrupted me, but then I disagreed with that since I felt rather badly about having interrupted you at the cemetery."

"Oh, but sir, you didn't. It was lovely . . . I mean, well it was nice meeting somebody who knew Jake. My brother. But you didn't interrupt me. Not at all!"

"Are you from far away?" he asked. "Like maybe California or back East?"

"Or maybe Europe?" she said with a lovely smile. "I—"

"Oh, are you from Europe?" And then he swiftly covered by saying, "Oh, I've interrupted you again."

"No you haven't. Not at all! In fact, I should have explained to you that I'm actually not from Europe. In fact, I've never even been there. Or anywhere, I mean, in Europe."

"Then you're from . . ."

"Ohio. Upper Sandusky, Ohio. Have you ever been there?"

They had slowed their walk as their conversation speeded up. And they were at the edge of the town now.

"No, I've never been to Ohio," the Gunsmith said. "But it must be nice there."

She stopped suddenly and facing him said, "Why? Why do you think it might be nice in Ohio? Especially if you've never been there?"

"Well, I don't know. I guess I've heard that it was nice in Ohio."

"Well, it is. In point of fact it is." She paused.

"In . . . uh . . . yes, well I'm glad of that."

"I'm a school teacher," she said. "That's why I sometimes speak in such a fancy way."

"I think it's very nice, the way you speak."

"Interesting. What do you do?"

"Do? Oh, I'm a gunsmith."

"Gunsmith! How devilishly interesting!" And she flushed. "I mean, after all, guns and gunfighting. One hears about such things. Back east one hears such stories about gunfighting and all. Have you ever had occasion to shoot anyone?"

"By the way," he said, stopping suddenly on the narrow trail—and ducking that particular question.

"My name is Clint. Clint Adams."

"Clint? Is that short for Clinton?"

"I think so. I mean yes, it is."

"I see. My name is Kimberly. People call me Kim."

"Kim? Kimberly?" He said the words carefully, testing them on his tongue. "They both sound good to me," he said.

"I like the name. It was my grandmother's name."

They had started to walk again.

"Do you plan to be in Landers for any amount of time?" he asked.

"Well, I only came to pay my respects to Jake. And also I . . ." And here she stopped as he saw the tears well in her eyes.

The next moment he had his arm around her, comforting her as she sobbed.

At last words began to come. "I'm sorry. I am truly sorry, Clint, or, Clinton. I mean, I was doing well—at least I thought so, and then when you asked me how long I was going to be here I realized the horrible way Jake . . ." Her voice trailed away.

"They told you everything?" he asked softly.

"They sent a wire. And I came. They said he'd been killed. When I got here I talked with some law person. A policeman, I guess."

"The sheriff, I reckon," Clint said. "Sheriff Steiner."

"That's the name. And he said someone, somebody had shot Jake. And they were hoping to find out who and catch him. . . ."

Again he had his arm around her and she was sobbing uncontrollably. He simply waited, trying to soothe her with a word now and then until at last she drew away from him. She took out her handkerchief, which was only a little larger than the palm of her hand, and began dabbing at her eyes until finally she had control of herself again.

"I am so sorry. I didn't expect that. And I'm sure you didn't. But thank you, Mr., er—Clinton for your kindness, sir. And if you're ever in Upper Sandusky, Ohio, my aunt has an extra room. You'd be most welcome."

And before he could say anything more she had turned and was running toward the town, her brown hair flying behind her.

He almost started after her, but stopped. And he stood where he was for maybe a whole minute before he started walking toward the town and his hotel. He was feeling completely thrown by the delightful adventure. And he realized that it had been a while since anyone—and there had been some beautiful and very passionate ones too—had affected him quite like Miss Kimberly Shore of Upper Sandusky, Ohio.

NINE

About a day's ride to the southwest of Landers, Fort Larrabee squatted on the high, rolling prairie. The army thus dominated one of the higher points of land which gave the command an unobstructed view for a good quarter mile in all directions.

Built of heavy timber, tar paper, prairie sod, and supported with a foundation of solid earth, Larrabee stood immovable against the winter freeze, summer heat, Indian attack, and possibly even the ravages of time. The fort was a day's ride east of the mountains and it guarded a large area, an area vital to the westering of the white man, and the push of the transcontinental railroad.

Clint Adams mounted up early; yet not so early that the hostler, Quince, wasn't already mucking out the stables and fussing around the livery. He even talked to his "boarders," of which there were quite a few: two chunky bay horses, a sorrel mare, and two white geldings.

Clint could see that the old boy had something on his mind, and he wondered if he was going to hear about it. He didn't have to wonder for long.

When he finally spoke, it was to the Gunsmith's back, for Clint's attention had suddenly been caught by something interesting.

"Studyin' the sorrel there," observed the old man. He cleared his throat and spat heavily in the direction of the mare who was standing in her stall, chomping on oats that had been put in her box.

"Hmmm." The Gunsmith was right up close to the sorrel now, rubbing her neck to calm her, scratching up around her ear.

"Light ain't more'n halfway good in here," Quince said as he took out his plug of tobacco and his clasp knife and cut himself a generous mouthful. "But I reckon you can notice what I seen."

He was thinking of that scene now as he came into view of Fort Larrabee.

"Didn't do a very good job of getting rid of that paint, did they?" Clint had said as he came out of the stall. "You see it, did you?"

"Mister, I just shovel the shit in this here hotel."

"Gotcha." And the Gunsmith stood very still, listening, with his eyes on the hostler. His voice was almost inaudible as he said, "I'll be riding out. Want to take a look around the North Fork." And as he spoke, he kept his eyes on Quince and tilted his head just a little. Quince replied by shaking his slowly.

"They come in 'bout an hour ago," he said, his voice almost inaudible.

"The Blackjack boys?"

The old man spat furiously in the direction of a scampering pack rat. "Naw, it was George Washington an' his girlfriend, fer Chrissakes."

And Clint had a great deal of difficulty to keep from laughing. "Glad to catch you in a good mood," he'd said.

"Mister, I allow as how you better take that big black hoss of yours elsewheres."

"How come?"

The old man remained silent.

But the Gunsmith pursued it. "Same bugger who was interested before?"

The old man nodded, sniffing as he did so.

"They'll be back." His words were almost a whisper.

Clint tried again. "You know them, do you?"

The old man was silent, hawking and spitting loudly as he turned and headed toward the back of the livery.

Clint led Duke out of his stall, checked him, and rubbed him down with the cloth that was hanging over the side of the stall. He worked quickly, yet deliberately, careful with each step in the saddling, and talking softly to his friend as he worked. It only took a few moments to get the horse ready for the long ride that was coming.

When he was finished he waited. Standing beside Duke he checked his six-gun, then squinted toward the door of the livery through which early morning light was coming.

" 'Bout ready, are ye?" The hostler's grainy voice was the only sound in the big barn.

Clint didn't answer. He had been leading Duke to the open doorway and now stopped and stood still for a moment, listening.

Beside him the horse wasn't making a sound.

Silence. Then he heard it again, the sound of someone breathing. Now he could even smell the man, his sweat and tobacco, as a breeze suddenly sprang up. Then he heard the thud of something dropping from inside the barn.

He turned, dropping into a crouch, as the first shot shattered the silence. He drew his Colt—swift as silk, the old man told him later—and shot his would-be assassin right between the eyes.

In the next second he ducked and threw himself sideways away from the open door as he heard the hostler cry out a warning. Two shots rang out, almost overtaking each other, and the Gunsmith fired again at the movement he sensed more than actually saw in the darkness inside the barn.

A cry of pain and surprise told him his score. Then in the next moment he heard the drumming of hooves out back of the livery as whoever was left of the failed bushwhacking took off.

"Mister! Mister!" Quince was almost crying with anguish as he came limping toward the Gunsmith. "I didn't know they was there! The sonsofbitches. They fooled me. I am swearing it, mister. I wouldn't have set you up like that!"

"Leave it," the Gunsmith said as he reloaded the Colt and dropped it into its holster. "Who were they?"

"Dunno their names. But I seen them around town, mostly in O'Toole's." The old man was gasping from lack of breath, excitement, and, it had seemed to Clint, fear.

He had let it go at that, except to ask if the man who had been interested in Duke was one of them.

"Not from what I saw, mister. But I didn't see much, I'll swear to that." The old man was shaking. Maybe not so much from fear, Clint finally decided, as from the strain on his aged body. More than likely they had roughed him up a good bit.

"I'll be heading for Larrabee," Clint told him.

"You mind that they'll be on your back trail?" the old man asked, squinting at him.

"About as much as I mind the weather—what I can do about it?" the Gunsmith answered. "I know they'll be there. From now on. And, as a matter of fact," he added. "From before."

"They been there all along, huh?"

"Sometimes close enough to shake hands," the Gunsmith said, and with an almost invisible nod he kneed Duke and pointed north.

He saw precisely where they had picked up his trail, just after he'd crossed Crooked Woman Creek and skirted the big butte where he saw the old remains of what at cursory glance looked like an old wagon train wipeout. He could see that the action had taken place at least a month ago. He paused now for a second look, but he still saw nothing that would tell him anything other than the fact that a few had died in the engagement; a few on both sides, red and white.

Now as he rode up in full view of the fort, he noted how well situated it was. The army had a clear view in all directions. He had been told that the military was a mounted infantry outfit. That is, not regular cavalry, but mounted foot soldiers.

On an impulse that suddenly struck him, he decided not to ride straight in to the fort, but to skirt the open area leading up to the army buildings, just to familiarize himself. It was a move that he generally favored; he preferred to thoroughly check the area he was going to visit before he actually arrived at his destination. He had certainly done so before riding into Landers, and he had learned a good bit of helpful material.

He decided to do the same here before riding into the fort. Nothing of special interest had appeared to him, and yet somehow he felt something tugging at him, something in a corner of his mind that he had actually seen but not really taken in.

The Gunsmith knew the feeling well. Instinct, a sixth sense, he told himself. Hell, it didn't matter what he named it, it was there and by God he knew he had better listen to it.

And it was there. It was right in front of him!

He had ridden wide of the fort, keeping away for the time being, with this sense of something out of tune. He rode Duke into the stand of cottonwoods and at last onto a thin game trail that led up into the high timber and eventually into the rimrocks. He realized he had found a place that would show him the entire army camp. Maybe that was what he needed, a different, longer view of the place—a physical picture that was not the usual horizontal one seen head-on. Here he had found a place where he could see not just the front or side, but the fort as a whole.

Knowing now that he had made the right decision, he kneed Duke into a slightly quicker walk, but still not letting him break into a canter. The big black was always eager, always willing to go for more, and Clint again and again had to hold him down. It was one of the many things he appreciated about his friend Duke: his willingness.

Presently, hidden from view of the army's fort they rode silently through thick stands of hemlock, spruce, pine, and fir, finally gaining the stony trail that led to the top of the great rocks. Breaking suddenly out of a stand of yellow pine, he found himself in a clear meadow, the whole sky holding himself and his horse right there, as though by a great hand.

And suddenly he saw right before him, halfway across the meadow, a huge bull elk accompanied by seven cows. They had been grazing, but now all raised their heads. Then, as though by some signal known only to themselves, they broke into a run across the lush meadow and into the trees on the far side, well away from the intruder, veering at the edge of the trees just before disappearing.

Smiling, Clint looked at the sky, thinking how the elk and other wild animals had such an extraordinary sense of what was around them; they always knew what was friendly, what was hostile.

He looked at the sky again, reading it. The light was rapidly waning. He realized that the meadow was on one side of a wide, deep valley off to his right, with the fort to his left.

Seeing grain in some horse droppings he knew that riders had been there; likely army, but certainly not Shoshone.

Slowly he cut across the meadow, wondering what the elk had seen that caused them to swerve as they fled away from the meadow. He had just crossed the meadow and ridden through a narrow stand of spruce to the edge of a second clearing when he saw the dead carcass of a buffalo.

Dismounting, he saw that the animal had not been dead long. It had been gutted. Its tongue had been taken and the entrails were spread about.

He squatted for a closer look, "It doesn't look good," he said aloud to Duke as he often did when thinking something over. "Hunh. Funny they left the hide." He stood up quickly, and walked soundlessly as he usually did on the trail, moving to where some entrails lay a few feet away.

"Shit!, Look here!"

He was looking down at the pile of guts, but especially at a white spot. Now, reaching into the entrails, he lifted out what looked at first like a piece of fat. It was the size of a large pill. "Strychnine," he muttered, still half to himself, half to his horse, who had shied away from the corpse and was moving his ears about nervously and blowing his nostrils.

Suddenly his eye caught some tracks. At first he thought it might be coyote. Somebody could be poisoning coyotes for their pelt. But the print wasn't a coyote's. Nor was it a wolf. It had to be a dog; he was damn sure it was.

The tracks were clearly recent. He was squatting, studying them. If it was a dog it could be an Indian dog, for there was a tipi town right next to the fort. Or it could be a soldier dog, but he doubted that.

Recent, but how recent? Studying the tracks he figured a day old. He looked up at the sky. No vultures. He felt pretty sure the dog had got some poison. If it was an Indian dog that could be big trouble. But why? Why would even the most brash wolfer be that stupid? And besides, the wolves had just about disappeared from this part of the country, he knew. The wolfers had killed off almost every one. For a while it had been a whole new industry, with wolfers swarming all over the place. But then suddenly—or so it seemed—the wolves like the buffalo, were gone, and with them the men who poisoned them. And that had been quite a while back. It made the present event mysterious. But more than that, it made it extremely dangerous. And he suddenly had the very strong feeling that somebody was indeed trying to stir up trouble with the Indians; in this case, the Shoshone.

Mounting Duke, he headed back toward the army fort. He was not happy at all to think about what might happen now. And maybe the

Shoshone already knew about the poison. He was pretty certain that they must. Their reservation wasn't far, he knew. And so it came back to that again—that somebody, some person or persons were trying to make trouble with the Indians. Why? Thinking about it as he rode back the way he had come, and then branched off toward Fort Larrabee, he suddenly felt a tension going through his body. If what he was speculating on happened to be true, then it was clear that somebody was trying to get Indian land. Why else stir up trouble with the tribes? And his thoughts went immediately to the Northern Pacific.

He decided to not ride to the fort directly, but to swing around the big butte by Buffalo River and the great chain of box canyons that paralleled a couple of miles of the south fork. He knew that track had recently been laid there and he was working on a hunch. Fifield Wister's words came back to him, remembering how the newspaperman had claimed the railroad—notably the Northern Pacific—was bilking the public, the government, and of course the native tribes through whose land they were running their rails.

Wister had told him of a narrow escape—one of many, he'd added—on the Northern Pacific. A bridge over Bitter Creek, just east of Green River, built upon abutments of soft sandstone, had crumbled away under a train that was filled with travelers. The engine, tender, and express car crashed into the creek and the passenger car, which was loaded with men, women, and some children, was only saved by a stringer of the bridge catching the coach's roof and holding it suspended over the brink. One passenger was killed and several were injured to varying degrees. The ironic point, however, or so it seemed to the Gunsmith, was that the bridge, as well as two other bridges in the vicinity, had been examined only the day before and had been pronounced unsafe! No one could say why the railroad didn't shut down those routes.

"There are those who claim the Northern Pacific's track is not only dangerous, but the worst that some of the inspectors have traveled over. Some of the deficiencies include unsafe bridges, tunnels not wide enough, the tracks not properly aligned, the roadbed not leveled—and not of the required fourteen-foot width. There were also crossties sunk in a bed that was not ballasted. Moreover, the ties were put down irregularly. However, one of the principal objections was the fact that the ties were soft white pine, when they were required by government construction standards to be of oak or other hardwood timber." Fifield Wister had gone on to read from the report he'd taken from his pocket when Clint was in his office. He noted that it was predicted that the white pine would quickly rot, thus requiring replacement of some thousands of ties. "And not to mention," Wister had continued, "the enormous danger to life and limb." He had worked himself into anger at that point and had continued to relate to Clint Adams a number of other mischievous incidents that not only would endanger the lives of the public but would cost even more money than the government had already bilked and handed over to the railroads.

Well, he reflected, there was not much new in this sorrowful situation, but it did verify the thoughts he'd been having about Landers and Cecil Dunbellamy and his crowd—or rather, gang.

It was just working in this way—what he sometimes called puttering—that the Gunsmith arrived at what he considered a reasonably true picture of the situation regarding Landers, the Northern Pacific, and the murder of both Jake Shore and Wayne Behrens.

He decided then and there that he needed nothing more to make up his mind as to the motives of Cecil Dunbellamy and the Northern Pacific.

He had completed his projected tour of that section of land just north and east of Fort Larrabee, checking the railroad and at the same time deciding what to do about the strychnine he'd found in the buffalo carcass.

The sun was just reaching the horizon when he rode into Fort Larrabee and gave his report to the commanding officer; Captain H. H. Warner.

Herbert Henderson Warner was a grizzled officer of the Union Army who had been shipped west—or so the gossip had it—because of his severe and industrious predilection for alcohol. But he was stone sober when the Gunsmith told him what he had discovered, and at the same time suggested that something be done to handle that situation pronto before Little Hawk, the chief of the Shoshone camp about two miles north of the fort, decided possibly to retaliate.

"I suggest, if I may, Captain, that Little Hawk be advised of what has happened, and indeed may be happening in other areas of South Fork."

The captain sniffed, blinked, and pursed his lips, the upper of which supported a brisk mustache. He regarded his visitor calmly.

"Mr. Adams, I must say it's good of you to inform the army of the poisoning of the buffalo up on the north slope, but happily we are already investigating certain other infractions of the treaty with the Shoshone. I am obliged to you, sir, for doing your duty in reporting here."

Something in the tone, the vibration, of the captain's little speech caught Clint Adams' attention. He wasn't yet quite sure what it was, but something rang through him, telling him to go easy.

"I had already planned to visit you, sir, to inquire about Jake Shore."

The captain's wiry eyebrows rose. "Oh, you knew Shore, did you, Mr. Adams?"

"I did, Captain."

"He did some scouting for us. For me." He paused, clearing his throat. "A good man, sir. A good man. A bit overzealous at times. I might add, and though enthusiasm can be a useful quality in civilized circumstances, out here with the natives, especially the Shoshone, let me add, it is better to go cautiously. And I'm afraid Shore stirred up a lot of ill-feeling amongst the local settlers. Fact, he was accused rather roundly—and I might add, rightly—of leaning rather heavily toward the . . . well, views of Little Hawk. That's to say that he for some reason that totally escapes me, felt the Indians—the Shoshone in particular—were getting a rather bad treatment at the hands of the army, and the settlers. And from Washington, in fact. And then . . . well, enough of that. It's tragic what happened to him, but there it is. There it is." He stood up suddenly, and held out his hand.

"It's good of you to come by, sir. I won't offer to give you more of my time for I'm due out on parade in five minutes, and following that I'll be scouting the northwest boundaries of Little Hawk's people. Not personally, of course, but I shall be occupied with . . . shall we say, the sensitivity—yes, the extreme sensitivity—of handling this situation. Especially now that we have further evidence—yours—of the poisoning. Matter of fact, the Shoshone had already lost a couple of their dogs. Pretty poor-looking beasts, the Indian dogs, and so no great loss. But we don't want any trouble from it!" And he stepped briskly around his desk and to usher Clint Adams to the door of his office.

"Oh, by the way, let me say again how sorry I am not to be able to afford you more time. As I said, duty. However, do go to the commissary and ask for Sergeant Billbow who's in charge and he will see that you get something to eat and drink." He chuckled—that was the only word Clint Adams could think of to describe the sound that came out from under his whiskers—and patting his guest on the arm, showed him the door.

As Clint stepped outside, the captain had an afterthought. "We're in a kind of disarray right now, because tomorrow we have a field exercise. Something I've inaugurated myself, to deal with the tribes—but should you wish to stay longer, then just let the sergeant know."

And touching his wrinkled brow with his forefinger he walked briskly away, leaving the Gunsmith with the unique feeling of having dealt with a sneaky schoolboy who thought he was getting away with something.

Ten minutes later he had mounted Duke and was on his way back to Landers. His visit had accomplished more than he'd bargained for. And he knew that he had plenty of work cut out for himself.

He took his time riding back to Landers, well aware that he had made a move that would definitely expose him to whoever it was working with Dunbellamy and the Northern Pacific. Of course, there would be strong factions, and powerful individuals behind Dunbellamy, people back East, people in Cheyenne, and it seemed presently, at least one man in the United States Army. Of course he had no proof. Actually, he didn't necessarily feel that proof was needed, or even useful. He knew that proof wasn't going to stop the avalanche of Cecil Dunbellamy's game. The Gunsmith knew without the least grain of doubt that the big steal was on, and he was most happily confident of the fact. He didn't know who or what group was at the helm; or even if there was a concentrated, direct, single plan; or whether, on the other hand, there were several people or groups in the action, like coyotes on a buffalo carcass. He was again reminded of the strychnine.

Well, by God, Jake and Wayne had sure been on to something. And so was he himself. It gave him pause, realizing that by now he had to be a marked man. Indeed, he might well be used as an example for any other foolish men who might try to question the validity of the theft, murder, and rape of the frontier by those men with the soft white fingers who knew so much and were so capable of counting money and snapping fingers with demands, or simply folding into silence in the face of inquiry. Dirty hands, dirty men, he was thinking as he dismounted at the livery after what had seemed not too long a ride. He then stripped Duke, who was ready for water, oats, hay, a rubdown, and maybe, the Gunsmith thought, even some words.

For, as was his custom, he had discussed his thoughts and notions a great deal with the big black gelding on his way back to Landers. And now, he saw the picture clearly.

It had not been easy to see it clearly, for there appeared to be so many different factions involved—the railroad, the land and grazing acreage, the various ranches, even the army, and not to forget the town.

Well, he thought, maybe that was how a country had to grow. A frontier like this one. Hard, but young and tough, and it was that youth and toughness that would make a man or break him.

Yes, he had done the right thing deciding to help Wayne, and also Jake. Those two had put themselves on the line—and it turned out to cost them their lives. He, Clint Adams, though not deep friends of either one of those men, still had worked with them separately, and he understood now that in a certain way the three of them had a similar feeling about the land and the people in it.

Clint Adams was no sentimentalist, but it galled him to see the slickers working through twisted interpretations of the law. With their power and money, they pushed the little people around, screwing the immigrants, and lying and cheating whole families who had, through the most severe conditions, finally made it to what the operators called "The land of plenty," only to find that they had been cheated.

He felt good then. He felt good as it all cleared in him, and his anger subsided. It was no good to be angry. An angry man was dangerous to lots of people, but mostly he was dangerous to himself. The Gunsmith felt himself relax, really relax as he dumped oats into the Duke's feed box and started up Main Street. It was evening, and he was going to stop at Jug's Barber Emporium and have a bath and, yes, maybe a shave. The evening lay ahead, and he needed to be fresh, alert, and mostly, he needed to be right with himself.

It was a tough one. But that was just what made it so good.

TEN

He was on the late side reaching the dining room in The Wrangler's Rest. But he had taken his time with the shave and bath. And he felt refreshed. At the same time, he somehow felt that his luck was in. Whatever that meant. In any case, he shortly found out. For his "luck" happened to be sitting all alone at a table at the far end of the dining room.

Not a man to hesitate under such circumstances, the Gunsmith went straight as an arrow to his objective. She'd had her back to the entrance of the room and so hadn't seen him enter. He decided to surprise her.

"I wonder if you'd like to join me?" he said as she looked up in surprise. "Or may I join you? Or . . . ?" And he looked at the chair opposite her, "Or perhaps you already have company?"

"Or," she said slowly with a smile that delighted him, "Or, Mr. Adams, why don't you sit down? I have only just ordered. A steak. I am very hungry. How about you?"

"I'm very hungry too," he said, seating himself. "Uh—would you like some nice French wine?"

"Oh, that's a wonderful idea. I'd love some nice French wine."

When he had given his order he said, "I am very glad I ran into you. I've been up at Fort Larrabee inquiring about your brother. Nothing you don't know already. He was doing some investigating for the government, I believe, and anyway, the captain there was sorry to hear the news, and passed his wishes on to you."

For a moment, she lowered her head and looked down at her hands. When she looked up he saw the tears forming in her eyes, and regretted mentioning Jake.

"You are a very thoughtful man, Mr. Adams."

"Please call me Clint."

"Clint."

"What'll I call you?" he asked, smiling at her.

"What would you like to call me?"

"I like Kim and I like Kimberly. I can't make up my mind about it, I guess."

"Well . . ." She leaned her elbows on the table, holding her hands together. Then she opened her fingers wide. "Well, you could call me Kim-Kimberly, or Kimberly-Kim. But then I can foresee that you would have the difficulty of possibly not knowing which Kim to start with—Kim for Kim or Kim for Kimberly. And so you . . . well you see—maybe you'd better think of some other name."

And they were both laughing.

By the time they reached dessert they still hadn't decided on the name situation. But by then it didn't matter.

"Would you like to take a stroll?" he asked. "It's a lovely evening."

"I think that would be great. And I've got a solution to your problem."

"You mean . . . ?"

"About your name, or rather, about my name. Your use of my name."

"Yes. So what have you decided?"

"I think the honorable thing, the sensible, most intelligent approach to this weighty question is simply to call me one name on one day and the second name on the second day, and simply alternate. Like that." And she laughed and nodded her head at him like a child who had just answered a knotty question correctly.

"There's just one small problem that I foresee here," he said.

She leaned forward on her elbows, her fingers laced together in front of her face. "And that is . . . ?"

"How to start. Shall we start with Kim and then go to Kimberly, or the reverse? I mean, I want to do the right thing, as those English dudes are so fond of saying."

She was laughing, shaking her head as she lowered her arms and leaned forward a little. "I don't know about the English dudes," she said. "Who are they?"

"The rich English who come out to the West

to ride and shoot and hunt and rough it, and all that sort of thing. Actually, there are some very nice ones."

"I've got it!"

He stared at her. "Got what?"

"How to solve your great problem."

He leaned forward, looking right into her lovely brown eyes. "How? Tell me, please. I have to know. I won't rest until I discover the answer, the secret . . ."

"You close your eyes."

"All right. Closed."

"Keep them closed. No cheating now."

"Gotcha."

"Now then let your mind go blank. Take a long breath."

"Gotcha," he said again. And he took a deep and long breath.

"Let it out slowly."

"Done."

"All right. Now your mind is a complete blank."

"Right."

"Is it?"

"Is it what?"

"Blank. Completely blank."

"It is."

"Good. Very good. We will just wait a moment." She paused. And then she said, "Tell me which name comes first to your mind."

"Mary."

"Mary!"

"That's what you asked. The first name that came to my mind. I had a sister named Mary. Or at least that's what she told me her name was."

"Open your eyes."

He did so, fighting to suppress his laughter.

"All right. You win. You can call me Mary."

He leaned back. "You still want to take a walk?"

"I believe that would be very nice, sir."

"Mary," he said, turning the name over in his mind as he said it.

They had reached the door of the dining room and stood for a moment just inside the lobby.

"I didn't ask you if you were staying here at the Wrangler, or just using the dining room," he said.

"I'm a guest here. And you?"

"Same."

They were outside now and the stars were spread all over the sky or so it seemed to Clint Adams. Without saying anything they began walking down the street. Yet he didn't feel as relaxed or secure now as he wished to be. Not only for his own welfare, but for the girl too.

They had reached the end of the walkway and he stopped and turned toward her. "It's pretty dark down there, and there are some rough boys about. I think it would be better for you to be inside."

"Very well."

They turned and walked back to the hotel. They had fallen silent, but although he didn't find it uncomfortable, at the same time it was at a place where he was not quite at ease.

When they each took their key from the room clerk, he said, "What floor are you?"

"Second."

"Ah, me too."

He followed her up the stairs, aware that the man at the desk was watching. Well, that was the way it was. Everybody was always watching somebody else, it seemed. And he felt better with that thought.

At the landing he said, "Which way?"

She nodded to the right. "Where are you?"

He nodded to the left.

And then he had his arm around her waist and was kissing her on the mouth.

She responded instantly, and his erection sprang to immediate attention as he held her tight, and their mouths opened to each other and their tongues began to work.

Without another word he had led her to his door, unlocked it, and they were inside.

"Phew," she said, touching her hair and smoothing her dress.

"Gee, that decision was almost as hard as picking what name I was going to call you."

"Hmm," she said, looking up into his eyes with a smile.

And slowly he began to undress her.

In moments they were naked, standing under the shaded light, for he had tossed his shirt over the back of the chair which was by the bed, so that the coal-oil lamp would not shine too brightly. Marvelous shadows were cast on the wall of the room as he approached her naked body with his stiff member leading right between her legs. And she was straddling it, soaking wet, and wiggling on it, bringing him such delight that he was sure he wouldn't be able to stand up another minute.

Then he brought her down on the bed, her legs spreading as his hand covered her soaking bush. She grabbed his rigid tool and her hand slid softly on his come which was all over both of them. He had not ejaculated, nor had she, but they were nevertheless soaking wet with their incredible desire.

"Oh, my God," she murmured, and almost cried out, but stopped herself in time. Her lips found his, their tongues sank deep into each other's mouths, and he rubbed his stiffness between her legs.

And then she was down on her back with her legs spread wide and up high as he mounted her with consummate skill. She squealed with utter delight while he thought he couldn't hold his load another second. Their thighs and bellies were smacking with the wetness as their hips drove at one another, and she sank her tongue deep into his mouth, reaching down with one hand to play with his balls, while her other hand teased the crack between his undulating buttocks.

He responded by riding her high, almost on her neck with her legs way up, pointing to the ceiling of the room, as she wiggled from side to side.

"I've got to have my feet down," she gasped, "so I can have a purchase on the bed."

He said nothing, gasping for breath as they wiggled and squirmed and plunged and withdrew, though never all the way out. He always kept the tip of his throbbing cock in her as she soaked him and soaked him, the come pouring down his thighs and onto his belly too.

And then they came, at the absolute, most exquisite peak of passion, they came together in perfect rhythm, and he gave it all—as did she.

He lay on top of her, still inside, both of them shuddering with the joy they had received, and were still enjoying. He lay right on top of her, his cock soft inside her, now getting smaller and moving out, though the rest of his body had not moved. And he could smell their come. Then they slept.

Presently, he felt her stirring beneath him, and her lips found his again, as his tool straightened, hardened, and began to move, stroking and wiggling until in a second it was totally erect and filling her. Her cunt gripped his cock and milked it with her delightful wiggling and the Gunsmith thought he would go totally out of his mind.

And they were riding each other wildly, beautifully in perfect rhythm, a dance of joy and bliss—no words could describe their feeling, their experience. Only faster and faster as she begged and sucked his tongue, and held his buttocks, gripped his buttocks as they squirmed, bounced, and fucked together all the way to the ultimate moment when they shot everything and then lay supine entwined in each other's arms and legs.

They slept. And later when they awakened they did it again. In the morning, the Gunsmith, half-asleep, half-awake, tried to remember how many times they'd done it. But he found he was having trouble because every time he thought of the score, he found he was erect and, as he told his lady friend right then and there, action speaks louder—and better—than words.

"Well then, we see what lengths the boys will go to—and are going to—to whip up the hysteria," said Fifield Wister as he walked to the window of his office and looked down into the main street of Landers.

"It sure looks like they're pulling out every stop and then some," said the Gunsmith. He snorted. "Cattle rustling, horse stealing, brand changing, stage and train holdups, and now by golly, they're working to get the Indians in on it."

"Once the army starts moving on it they'll declare a state of war and then . . ." Wister was standing at his desk, and now sat down. "Except, I don't figure how come they want the Injuns and the army locking assholes and making one helluva fandangle."

"That's easy," said the Gunsmith.

Wister snorted. "Easy! Easy, you say! How the hell does getting the whole of the damn army involved in a fight with the tribes make anything easier for anybody! You answer me that and you you can go to the top of the class. Shit, man, you can take over the damn class. It's crazy! Just Goddamned crazy!"

"Crazy like a coyote, my friend."

"Tell me. Tell me, Mr. Genius Man!" He was leaning up against his desk, with his fingers extended, the tips just touching the mahogany.

Every inch of the man was indignant, Clint could see.

"It's simple. With the army engaged in quieting an Indian revolt, maybe even a small war, the town won't be able to expect any help in establishing law and order here, in Landers." Clint opened his hands in an offering gesture. "Simple. Easy."

Fifield Wister's mouth dropped open, his eyes almost bugging out of their sockets with indignation. "Then tell me how the hell that's going to . . ." He was almost shouting the words in his exasperation. Then suddenly he stopped. He froze, stock still as he saw what the Gunsmith had been trying to tell him all along.

"Holy Mother of God!" And Clint Adams realized how moved the man had to be to resort to the accent and expression from the Old Country, Fifield Wister being one of those earlier immigrants from Ireland who had insisted in rising above the epithets of "Potato-eater," "Shanty Irish," and so on. "Plain as the nose on me face!" he intoned, falling even further into the brogue.

The Gunsmith watched him smile and redden in the cheeks, while his eyes lit up. He could tell that Fifield Wister felt pretty good, pretty *damn* good, coming home to the Old Sod! And, Clint smiled to himself, understanding that even though Wister had become an educated man, taking on the role of a writer, an editor, even a sage, he was a lonely man. And in a moment of crisis he'd had the good fortune and, yes, maybe the courage to return to his roots.

"You want to help this town, don't you?" Clint said as his host sat down.

"I do." He had his elbows on the desk now and his chin was in his hands. "I do want that," he said. "It's a good town, and it's got good people. Good stock. Landers doesn't need the likes of Killigan and his gang, and Dunbellamy and the sonsofbitches who be backing him!"

"And the council—that is, Dunbellamy—will ask for the army, but the army will be busy with the Indians. So a local bunch of law enforcers will take over the town to restore law and order."

"You have hit the nail you know where," said Fifield Wister. "Killigan and his boys will be the law."

"Will be—or are?" said Clint as the sound of firing in the street became suddenly louder.

Wister crossed to the window, but kept himself out of sight as he studied the street below.

"They'll be coming after you," he said now. "So you're the Gunsmith!" He turned back from the window. "Are you going to help us, Mr. Adams?"

"I hope to," Clint said. " 'Course, if you've a mind to want me."

Wister was grinning. "That is a foolish question. I consider not to have heard it." He laughed, reaching for the bottle.

But Clint held up his hand. "I'll pass this one up. If I'm going to be helping you I'm going to have to have my wits about me. That means I have to be sober, sharp, fast, etcetera. In fact, all those points that the readers of your newspaper pieces expect a gunman, a lawman, and likely a soldier even to have as part of his daily existence."

And the Gunsmith was grinning as he stood up. "When do you reckon Killigan'll make his move to take over? 'Course I know he'll have to get the sign from Dunbellamy."

"You're an observant man, Mr. Adams."

"True, but call me Clint."

"My friends call me Banks."

"Sounds like money," said Clint, and they both laughed at the joke.

Then Clint said, "I would guess pretty sure that the boys have got the town under control right now."

"Killigan and his vigilante boys." Wister remarked dryly.

"Dunbellamy and the Northern Pacific," the Gunsmith corrected.

" 'Course. Of course." And Fifield Wister ran the back of his hand across his mouth. "Of course," he added.

Clint Adams crossed to the window now and looked down into the street. "Well, I'd reckon it won't be long now."

"That looks like Killigan and some of his boys down there now," Wister said.

"Where does Steiner stand with it?" Clint asked. "Is he in the picture? Is he one of Dunbellamy's men? Or will he—or has he—sold out to the N.P. and Dunbellamy?"

Now a silence fell in the little office. Clint Adams, looking down into the street, while standing back and a little to one side of the window felt a nagging in a corner of his mind. He knew the feeling. It came when there was something he hadn't quite seen clearly, came with the feeling that there was something he'd been missing.

"Right now," Fifield Wister was saying, "there's only one way to stop this madness."

"How?" The Gunsmith had turned from the window.

Fifield Wister, the publisher, and editor-in-chief of *The Landers Bugle* drew himself up to his full height and looked gravely at the man known as The Gunsmith.

"How? How? You ask how?" And a smile broke on his face, but it wasn't humorous. "You ask how. The Gunsmith!"

And all at once the uneasiness that Clint Adams had been sensing seemed to tighten all the way through him.

"My gun is not a gun for hire, Mr. Wister. I keep telling people that; and I sometimes find it hard to make the point. I've used my gun, and as long as I live and am able I will continue to use it. But only as a last resort."

"But of course, of course! I didn't mean anything at all in the way of you going out there and shooting a couple of people. I meant that . . . well very simply, I meant only that we need you on our side. You see, when you suddenly appeared in Landers, as it were "out of the blue," as the saying goes, some of us thought you had been hired by Cecil Dunbellamy to take over—maybe even to run the Killigan boys. I've since seen my error, there, and I am sure, I know, that others have also seen that this was wrong." He paused, and seemed to Clint to be a little out of breath. Yet, every inch of the man seemed to be breathing apology and sincerity.

"Then how do you see me helping you?" Clint asked quietly.

Fifield Wister ran the palm of his hand around the back of his neck. He sniffed. He blinked, there was a trace of a smile in his eyes and at the corners of his mouth.

He said, "You can go down there and find Bowdrie Killigan and kill him."

The words fell into the small, cluttered office like a whole lot of unfired bullets. As though, Clint suddenly thought, those bullets were there for him to choose from. It was a crazy thought, not the kind of poetry he was given to. Yet there was sense to it, he felt. And again, for the briefest moment he felt the sense of strangeness that had swept him only minutes earlier.

The silence lengthened.

And then at last Wister said, "I am sorry if I put it badly. I was really only asking for your help, and certainly not as a . . . well, as a hired gun. Only as a man who does know how to use a gun, and who is famous for his integrity and his honesty and guts. I—I well, I sometimes get carried away when I see what these swine are trying to do to the frontier, and have done so, in fact. They've already ruined so much. And they want more. Their greed knows no boundaries!" He stopped, ran the back of his hand across his wrinkled brow, and gave the Gunsmith a small smile.

"Gotcha," Clint said. "I think we understand each other, and I do see the situation. I will try to help you, and the others. I will try to help Landers. I promise you that. After all, two good friends of mine died trying to do the same thing, you know."

"I do know. And I want you to know that you can count on me to help you all the way!"

They stood there facing each other as each took in the moment that had held them so forcefully.

"It will happen any day now," Fifield Wister said softly, his eyes on a corner of the room. "It can happen at any hour."

It was just as he said those words that they heard the gunshots, accompanied by the galloping horses and the shouts of people down in the street.

"That sounds like just exactly what I have been talking about," said Wister. And he turned to face Clint Adams.

But the Gunsmith had vanished. Fifield Wister was alone in his office.

ELEVEN

As the Gunsmith swiftly descended the stairs leading from Fifield Wister's office to the street, the image of Kimberly Shore flashed through his mind. He hoped she was somewhere safe inside. But that was all he could do about that. He had warned her, or rather cautioned her when they'd spent the night together, but he realized now he hadn't been as forceful about it as he could have been. But then he hadn't anticipated the speed with which the situation might come to a climax. For he had to assume now that the great noise in the street was Killigan in action; action inspired by Cecil Dunbellamy.

It all fit. And suddenly, stopping now inside the downstairs door leading to the street, from which he could still hear gunfire, the thought took him almost completely was that he had somehow overlooked something.

Instead of trying to slip out into the street quickly, so he could get a better view of the action, he paused, just inside the door. Wondering. There

177

was something he was missing. It just seemed that it was all a bit too pat, a bit too simply deciphered. And suddenly a question occurred to him. Was somebody setting up a situation where he, the gunsmith, would see it in a certain anticipated way; that is, the way that person, or persons wanted him to see it?

And again the thought jabbed at him that two good men—Jake Shore and Wayne Behrens—had already tried to do something about the situation in Landers and the surrounding country, and that those two good men were now dead. Murdered. Bushwhacked. Killed without a chance of defending themselves.

Suddenly a thunder of galloping horses swept down the street and past the door where he was standing. He was just inside, out of sight, but he could see clearly the hard, angry, wild faces of the riders. They had no masks, were making no attempt at hiding themselves.

So bold! So unafraid of any opposition! And then he realized what it was that he'd been missing. It was as clear as a cowbell now. They—or someone—were simply doing what they'd said they would do. Openly. As though it was absolutely the right thing, the lawful action to take. But of course!

And in the next moment he had stepped out onto the boardwalk and started to walk down the street in the direction of the livery. He had a sudden flash that he had better take a look at Duke.

Five minutes after he had walked into the livery, he realized he must be edgy. Duke was fine.

He had wanted to check him anyway, in case of a sudden need to get somewhere fast. It was always a good idea to have your back trail free and open.

He spent a few moments talking to the horse as he brushed him, rubbed him down, and checked his legs, and his shoes. Saw that he was in good shape and, in fact, ready to go wherever he was asked.

At the same time the Gunsmith was very much aware that he had been seen entering the stable. He was also wondering where Quince was. The old hostler hadn't answered when he'd called out his name. Well, he could be in the outhouse or maybe uptown on an errand.

Satisfied that Duke was ready for riding, he drew on his bridle, then his blanket, and, finally saddled him. The Gunsmith appreciated the fact that the horse did not swell his belly when he cinched him, so that later when he stepped into the stirrup to mount, the saddle would slip and he'd end up on his back, likely in a stack of horse-shit. It was a game they sometimes played. But maybe Duke knew that this particular moment was not a moment for fooling around and Clint Adams appreciated it.

He had just turned away from the horse and was stepping out of the stall when he heard the step outside the livery.

"Well, if it ain't his lordship the Gunsmith!" The sneering voice was instantly recognizable.

And then he saw the big man standing just to the side of the barn door, with the sun behind him. And he felt, more than saw the other three off to his left.

"We be lookin' for some posse to establish the law and the order in Landers," Killigan said, and his hard voice was steeped in laughter.

Clint Adams saw immediately that of course the four of them had been drinking hard.

"Isn't that the sheriff's job?" he said in a neutral tone of voice. Not far away were some other men, many of whom seemed armed, but they were keeping their distance.

"Sheriff's busy handlin' them Injuns up to Finders Creek. Seems them ignorant savages been runnin' amok. To hear folks who been up there tell of it. You gonna help us git them villains, Mr. Gunsmitty?" And he could hardly get the last word out for suddenly breaking into laughter.

Clint Adams looked at the onlookers' faces. There was laughter, and there was fear too. But they were there. The audience, the crowd that thrived on the laughter and fear and mostly the sense of crude, rude power that Bowdrie Killigan evoked.

"You gonna help or not, Gunsmitty?"

And that was it.

"Where is Quince?" Clint stood quietly and he spoke quietly. And he knew that it was the quiet that would provoke Killigan.

"Quince? Hah! Where is Quince?"

At this the group standing close to Killigan broke into raucous laughter. And the Gunsmith felt something quicken in his blood.

"You telling me that Quince is no longer with us, are you?" And his hard eyes were gripping Killigan. Hard eyes, but quick as silver. As he was himself. He could feel it flowing through him, the way it always did when he was right; that is to say when everything within him was where it was supposed to be. And everything was therefore true.

"Oh he's still with us," said the big man, and his sneer was as heavy as the laughter that pounded out of him. The crowd was right with him, right with the big bully—which was exactly how the Gunsmith wanted it to be.

He stood there, loose all the way through, yet with that current of energy he knew so well streaming all through him.

He had checked the rooftops quickly when he'd stepped into the street. And while he still saw no one on any of the buildings across from him, there were still alleys, and other possibilities. For instance the lumber wagon across the street and down to his left. Or any of the three alleys, all of which were in easy range. He wondered if maybe Wister might be covering him from his office. And then all at once he saw it all.

He saw the situation, saw it clear and whole. It was one of those moments when he felt his whole self alive, loose, but yet engaged at the same time. It was as though there were something quicker than thought in him, something that he *knew*.

In that moment he saw Killigan's eyes flick to the roof over his, Clint Adams' head, just a flick as though the sunlight had touched him.

But it was enough. For, Killigan was holding his hands way out to his sides; obviously he wasn't aiming to draw. But for the Gunsmith it was the giveaway.

And in the next breath he had dropped to the ground on his back, drawing as he rolled and was up facing the man who had crept up behind him. And he shot Fifield Wister right between the eyes. In the next breath he had again dropped, but this time to one knee, and shot Bowdrie Killigan in the throat.

It was over. None of the men standing by Killigan made a move, except those closest to where the big man had been standing moved their arms out to their sides, making sure that the man known as the Gunsmith could see they were out of it.

The Gunsmith was already on his feet.

"Unbuckle!" he snapped. "Every one of you. I mean right now!"

And they did it. None were faster than the three who had tried to dry-gulch him not so very long ago: Harold, Stacey, and Lennie.

"Where is Ed Steiner?" the Gunsmith demanded.

"I am here," said a voice at the back of the crowd, which now opened to allow the sheriff to pass through.

Ed Steiner was very pale, but he walked with a steady step.

"I guess you really do be that feller they call the Gunsmith," he said with an attempt at wry humor.

But it was a good thing to say, Clint decided. It showed him something more about Ed Steiner.

"You still want this town cleaned up?"

"Looks to me you done a pretty fair to middlin' job already, Mr. Adams. What about Cecil? You thought about him?"

"It depends what you and your town want, Sheriff. You asked me to help you clean the town. I have done my bit, I think. I believe you and them," he nodded toward the crowd, "can do it, but only if you want to." He paused, squinted at the weather, and then said, "If you want a decent town, and if you want the railroad, then get it—but get it on your terms. 'Course," he added, "that's up to you. I'll be moving on."

Not so very long after the shooting he said more or less the same thing to his friend Kim-Kimberly. He had decided to take the sensible way in the matter of which name came first, simply by using both forms alternately.

"The only trouble with that, Kimberly-Kim," he said later as they lay totally relaxed in each other's arms, "is that I have to remember which is first at the particular moment."

He was lying on top of her after their first round of passion, and he could feel her beginning to stir for more, as indeed he was himself.

"The only thing you have to do, Mr. Gunsmith, sir, is to know that first is where you are and second is what you do after. Got it?"

"I've got it right here," he said, pushing his rigid erection into her.

"My God," she whispered, digging her nails into his back and buttocks. "That thing you've got sticking into me is what comes next."

"That thing?"

"That loaded stick, mister."

"That's what I'm here for," he said. "Ready and willing."

"I'm so grateful it's always so ready," she whispered in his ear, and then licked him.

"I'm glad," he said, entering her high and deep. "After all," he added, "I dunno. But maybe that's why they call me the Gunsmith."

Watch for

GILA RIVER CROSSING

143rd novel in the exciting GUNSMITH series
from Jove

Coming in November!

If you enjoyed this book, subscribe now and get...

TWO FREE

A $7.00 VALUE—

If you would like to read more of the very best, most exciting, adventurous, action-packed Westerns being published today, you'll want to subscribe to True Value's Western Home Subscription Service.

Each month the editors of True Value will select the 6 very best Westerns from America's leading publishers for special readers like you. You'll be able to preview these new titles as soon as they are published, *FREE* for ten days with no obligation!

TWO FREE BOOKS

When you subscribe, we'll send you your first month's shipment of the newest and best 6 Westerns for you to preview. With your first shipment, two of these books will be yours as our introductory gift to you absolutely *FREE* (a $7.00 value), regardless of what you decide to do. If you like them, as much as we think you will, keep all six books but pay for just 4 at the low subscriber rate of just $2.75 each. If you decide to return them, keep 2 of the titles as our gift. No obligation.

Special Subscriber Savings

When you become a True Value subscriber you'll save money several ways. First, all regular monthly selections will be billed at the low subscriber price of just $2.75 each. That's at least a savings of $4.50 each month below the publishers price. Second, there is never any shipping, handling or other hidden charges—*Free home delivery*. What's more there is no minimum number of books you must buy, you may return any selection for full credit and you can cancel your subscription at any time. A TRUE VALUE!

J. R. ROBERTS

THE GUNSMITH